ENFOLD

Thornhill Trilogy 3

J. J. SOREL

EDITOR Red Adept Editing

CHAPTER ONE

AIDAN

ALL THE USUAL SUSPECTS were there, including the uninvited. One of those being my ex-fiancée, Jessica. She was the last person I wanted around. But there she stood, posing in her typical must-be-center-of-attention way. Her dress was so tight that I was certain she wasn't wearing any underwear. Not that she turned me on. If anything, Jessica repulsed me.

Instead, I gazed at my beautiful girl. She always managed to chase away my fears. Still, I couldn't help but wonder what Jessica was plotting. Those teasing green eyes of hers were filled with spite. That was plain to see.

Clarissa was bubbly and bouncy. Perhaps a little too bouncy for my liking. Privately, yes, yes, yes. I couldn't get enough of her curves. But not in public. I exhaled a jealous breath. What was a possessive man to do? That pretty, thin-strapped gown offered little support. And as I watched Clarissa smiling and chatting with the guests, I noticed that she had the attention of most of the males there.

Tabitha, who had her own collection of admirers, had her arm linked with my father's. They were in love. Or so Grant admitted to me, the day I returned from a work trip after I ran into him at the estate, where he'd been crashing all week.

Sara, his partner of ten years, had thrown him out. Which didn't surprise me. One-night stands, she could tolerate, but googly-eyed romance, that was another thing.

My father had a weakness for young blonde women, and Tabitha, who was thirty years younger, fitted his ideal woman perfectly. Although she wasn't my type, I was more than aware of her charms, and she didn't hide her attraction for my dad, given that she was all over him.

I warned him that she changed her men as often as her underwear. But he just laughed it off. I had to admit his eyes had a glow that I'd never seen on him before. At the time, I recognized it well enough. I'd seen that same relaxed, flushed look of satisfaction when seeing myself in the mirror.

Despite it being nice to see Grant happy, an uncomfortable tightness still sat in my gut. Evan was heartbroken. A situation I wish I hadn't been thrown into. It had gotten so bad that Evan, while stalking Tabitha, ran into them walking arm in arm on the street.

The story had it that in an instant, my father and Evan were in each other's face, puffing and swearing. Tabitha pulled them apart. Something told me my father would have come off second best.

After that incident, I met with Evan to discuss the situation. I found myself on a slippery path. It wasn't my thing to get involved in others' little fucked-up scenarios. But after a few beers at a dark and discreet bar, I loosened up and spoke to him about his jealousy. I told him that beating women was barbaric and unforgivable and that he needed help. I also mentioned that I had to sweet-talk Clarissa for days to keep him employed.

His dark eyes shone with regret. I could see Evan was a broken man. If anything, I felt sorry for him. We shook hands in the end. I reassured him that our friendship and working relationship would remain intact as long as he promised to stay away from Tabitha. And so, the saga ended there. Or at least, I hoped.

Being head of security, Evan was my top guy. He knew the system inside out. He was a tough wall of a man. The type of guy an empire like mine needed. Especially at that moment, with so many ghosts of my regrettable past shadowing me.

I could look after myself well enough. But hell, if anything happened to Clarissa, I hated to think what I'd do.

I'd even kill for her. I'd pay every dollar I owned to protect her. Without Clarissa, the successful version of me would crumble.

Somewhat obsessed by her addictive beauty, I gazed over at her again. She had that rosy complexion she got when engrossed in a conversation about art. Every day, I saw something new in her. My love for her just kept growing.

I thought about the line of a song I'd written the night before. *Like a magic tree, nourished by love and reaching for heaven, my love for you will grow on and on and on.* It was one of the many songs I'd written since meeting Clarissa. Of course, she was always the subject.

My love for her was so profound, I suddenly found myself thanking God for bringing Clarissa into my life.

The VHC art auction was a complete success. Every painting sold for well over the reserve. Clarissa had arranged the event to be held at an upmarket gallery, and everyone who was anyone in the art world had turned up. Chris was in his element, even if he behaved a little anti-social. But I could see that, with his badass attitude, he was having a ball while attracting attention at the same time.

As someone who preferred to observe rather than chat mindlessly, I hid in a corner.

Clarissa sashayed toward me.

"Hey, Princess. Come here and hold my hand. I'm getting insecure."

She giggled. "Oh, Aidan. I could say the same about you. You look gorgeous in those cream linen pants. All the women are finding it hard to speak."

I drew her tight and kissed her. "Well, I'm finding it hard to move, watching that luscious body of yours spilling out of that pretty dress."

Her large brown eyes sparkled. "Then I'm glad you wore loose-fitting pants." Wearing a sultry smile, she added, "You're very big, you know."

I frowned. "No, I'm not."

She leaned in and whispered, "I have nothing to compare you to, but you always manage to make me burn."

I couldn't help but grin. "Clarissa, it's because, sexy girl, your exquisite little pussy is seriously tight."

And so it went on, our lusty banter. By that stage, I wanted to grab her and take her somewhere dark so that at least my hands could feast on her warm curves.

We'd been together for four months. I couldn't believe how my heart, soul, and cock craved Clarissa to the point of urgency. It was an addiction that was as unnerving as it was exhilarating. I'd suddenly discovered what all the poets had been on about for centuries.

Chris nodded over at us.

The second half of the auction was about to start. *Cock-slinger Freak*, the painting of the night, and one that had everybody talking was about to be auctioned.

Roy was as nervous as they came. He'd approached me earlier, admitting that. I patted him encouragingly on the arm and told him that his bank account would soon look healthier. He nearly cried. Just that response alone had made all my efforts to help talented, fallen creatures worth it.

"Hey, guys." Wearing his characteristic sardonic grin, Chris was in his element. He rubbed his hands together. "This is it. I'm going to be sad to see it go. I'm almost tempted to buy it."

His focus remained fixed on Jessica, who stood on the other side of the room, mincing amongst the well-heeled and the arty-types who, in contrast, couldn't afford to pay their rent. The latter added color and were there predominately for the free liquor. I didn't mind. In many ways, I related to them more because deep down inside I was still that barefooted kid.

Clarissa, with that rare heart of hers, stopped me from throwing Jessica out earlier in the evening after she'd pranced through the door, light on clothing but heavy on self-entitlement with that haughty smirk. At least, she stayed away from me, despite those cat eyes stealing little glances that I either ignored or scowled at.

"Who's that chick?" Chris asked, cocking his head in her direction.

"That's Jessica. An ex. She's fucking trouble."

"Mm... my favorite type of woman," he rasped with a wicked curl of his lips.

"Which? Exes or troubled women?"

He snorted. "Both. The more fucked-up and desperate they are, the better they fuck." He slurred his words. His shoulder-length blond hair had not seen a comb for some time. He had heavy-lidded, stoned blue eyes, and slouched in a don't-give-a-shit way.

I didn't think I'd ever spoken to Chris once when he was straight. Regardless of that, he worked tirelessly. For me, the fact that Chris had a genuine desire to see his students succeed mattered most. What people did behind closed doors and to their bodies was their own business.

Perched on an easel, the canvas depicted ejaculating blood leaping out at the viewer in a brutal fashion. A gun, cleverly painted to resemble a penis, added to the visceral impact of the work.

It started at two thousand dollars, which I thought was too low, but Chris assured me that it would act as a teaser. I got that. The more bids there were, the more likely buyers would be inclined to compete.

During my short experience attending auctions, I'd observed how it brought out the competitive streak in the rich. For me, it was the love of the work that kept me bidding. Especially the Godward piece that I'd paid a tidy sum for. It never stopped astounding me the similarity between the reclining woman and Clarissa. The fact I hadn't met her at the time made my desperate need for that painting almost supernatural.

The bidding pushed along at a feverish pace. We were up to twenty thousand dollars when Clarissa squeezed my hand. It was exciting for me, too. I cast a glance at Roy, who sucked on his bottle of beer as if his life depended on it.

When it got to fifty thousand dollars, Chris turned and winked at me. I grinned back. He was a sonofabitch, but I liked his spirit.

It didn't surprise me when Jessica won the bidding at one hundred thousand dollars. By that stage, Roy had gone pale as he leaned against a wall.

I went to him. "Hey, well done, man."

He shook his head in disbelief. "I can't believe it."

"It's a great work, Roy. All of your art's great. This is only the beginning for you."

"The money will help set me up. That's for sure," he said, almost in a dream state.

"You can have access to the VHC anytime."

"Aidan, you would have to be the most generous guy on this planet. And what you've done at the Vets for everyone. You don't have to give me half of the money, you know. It should go to the center."

When Clarissa came to join us, Roy nodded with a quivery smile.

"The center will earn fifty big ones from your work alone. Think about that, Roy," I said with an encouraging nod. "Nothing motivates one more than a sale. It's yours. You earned it. You're talented. Embrace it."

Taking Roy's hand, Clarissa shook it. "Congratulations. It's a startling piece. Truly. I loved the way you stacked the paint in the foreground, while the background is so finely produced. The contrast's fabulous. That's what makes it original."

He nodded, his eyes warm and appreciative. "That was my intention. The blood thick and sculptural."

Chris shuffled over. "Hey, man. Good result." He hugged Roy. Something told me that Chris related to the broken former soldier in more ways than just his talent. I seriously hoped that Roy wouldn't catch Chris's bad habits, given that they were close.

We left them to it.

I needed a break from people so I led Clarissa away to the restroom.

"That was surprising," I said.

"It didn't surprise me. It's an extraordinary piece. I'm only disappointed Jessica bought it."

"I'm sorry that she made an appearance." I exhaled a slow, frustrated breath.

"It's not your fault, Aidan. This is a public event. I just get the feeling she bought it to show off. She'll probably throw it in a cupboard somewhere, never to be seen, which saddens me. The subject's heavy, and I probably couldn't keep staring at it, but it still deserves to be hung."

I nodded. "You're right, beautiful girl." I drew her close and held her. "Ah... that's better, some Clarissa magic. I almost feel myself again."

She pulled away and gazed at me with those sensuous dark eyes that made me melt. "Aren't you enjoying this?"

I shrugged. "You know me. I'm happier at home on the sofa. With you naked."

She giggled. "Aidan, you're incorrigible. I thought Tabitha and your father would've come. I invited them."

I puffed my cheeks and blew slowly. "The Red House gig's on tonight."

"What about Sara? Is she still in the band?"

"No, she left. My dad knows lots of musicians. It's a jam night, anyway."

"I'm so sorry. I liked Sara."

"Yeah, she's a good woman. She's the only woman my father's ever done the mileage with."

"I feel responsible, Aidan."

I brushed her cheek. "Hey, baby, you're not. If it weren't Tabitha, it would've been someone else. I spoke to my father the other day. He admitted he'd been depressed for a long time. He told me that meeting Tabitha had given him a new lease on life. I just wish Evan hadn't been involved. That's all. Something's simmering there. It worries me."

Alarm coated her eyes. "What? Do you think he'll cause trouble?"

"I think he'd like to. But Evan's business means more to him. I warned him not to go near her."

"What was his response?"

I shrugged. "He agreed. But it felt like something in him was dying to erupt. I recognize the signs well enough." I stared deeply into Clarissa's eyes. "If someone took you away from me, I'd go nuts."

"Men don't even register with me. They just blend in with the crowd." She stroked my arm. Her eyes hooded. Mm... I needed to get her out of there quickly.

Her face lit up. "Can we go to the Red House? I'd love to go."

I lifted the bodice of her dress in a lame attempt at covering her ballooning cleavage. "This is a bit low-cut for my liking. My cock loves it. But the trouble is I think other cocks love it too."

She giggled girlishly, making my dick stir as I pictured that pretty silk dress sliding down to her dainty feet.

"You know, Aidan, this has been an overwhelming success." She hugged me. "You're so clever for devising it."

"Not clever, Princess, just inspired by you." I twisted a strand of her silky hair around my fingers. "Do you want to go to the Red House?"

Her face brightened. "I'd love to."

"Okay, then. But only if we can get something to eat on the way. What do you say to a cheeseburger on the beach?"

She nodded. "I could eat one for sure, I'm hungry, and it's such a lovely night."

I nipped at Clarissa's swanlike neck. Her thick black hair tickled my nose, so I brushed it away. My hand lingered over it. It was soft and silken as I tucked it behind her ear. Her pretty elfin face gave me a shy smile. She was still bashful after all we'd done to each other. Her nipples were hard. And so was my cock. I leaned her against the wall. My hand traveled up her leg. Her panties were damp. "Clarissa, we need to go, now."

She floated along in my arm, and we left out the back without fanfare. My favorite type of departure.

I rummaged around the back of my car, looking for a sweater. I found one and held it up to Clarissa.

She scrunched her nose. "Oh, Aidan, I can't wear that."

"Well, I'm as sure as hell not going in there with your tits hanging out like that. And those nipples that could poke out an eye. Do they ever go down?"

"Not around you." She smiled seductively.

Hmm... good answer.

She pulled the sweater over her head, messing up her hair and making her look even sexier.

The garment swam over her little frame. Her little scowl made me laugh. Nevertheless, I rolled up the sleeves. "There, it doesn't look too bad."

"It looks ridiculous."

I held my chin and studied her. "You look hot."

"No, I don't." She rummaged around in the trunk and found a scarf. "How about this?"

I shook my head and chuckled, taking it off her. "Forget it. Come as you are. You'll just have every man in there salivating. That's all."

· · · ● · ● · ● · ●

As we walked to the rear of the building, I held Clarissa tightly against me. I was still flushed with endorphins from having made love. There was something special about fucking in a car with my girl straddling me, her delectable tits in my mouth, while she scratched into my arms and moaned sweetly while coming all over my cock.

I punched the number sequence and pushed the door. There were Bob and Jack, my trusty security guys to greet me. "Hey, guys. How's it going?"

"Yeah, good, Aidan. How are you? Long time no see."

"I'm great. I've just been busy." I flashed a smile at Clarissa.

After Clarissa greeted the pair, we headed down the hallway and discovered that the band was on a break.

Without thinking, I opened the door to the band room. Doubling back, I wished I'd knocked. My father had Tabitha balancing on his knees, his hand down her blouse as they smooched noisily.

Clarissa and I went to turn away when Grant, who was facing us, looked up. His glistening lips made me recoil. Tabitha quickly zipped up her jeans.

"Guys... great to see you here," my father said, jumping up.

Tabitha squealed with joy at seeing Clarissa.

"I think it's time you got a lock on this door," I said, creeped out at seeing my father with a woman young enough to be his daughter.

He was all smiles and light in mood, just as I'd seen him the other day— punching the air and blissed out. There was no doubt he was flying high, literally, for his eyes had that glassy film he got following a spliff.

We left the girls to it. They were lost in their weird little world, chatting and giggling. I had to admit it was heart-lifting to see Clarissa buoyant and giggly, acting like a schoolgirl. Although I could never trust Tabitha where men were involved, I understood their closeness. If it made Clarissa happy, it made me happy.

CHAPTER TWO

CLARISSA

AIDAN LIT UP THE stage with his handsome presence. With Grant by his side, both father and son had that rock-star allure about them. Biting his bottom lip, Aidan ripped out a tune, his back arched, his biceps flexed as his fingers ran up and down the fretboard. It was so carnal I imagined that was my body he was fluttering over.

With his pelvis thrusting against the back of his guitar, Aidan was a force of nature. His sexy allure was so thick it was splashing off the walls. I sensed a collective sigh from all the women in the audience. The atmosphere was awash with female hormones. How could it not be with Aidan looking like that, as if he were having sex with his instrument. Mm... I'd seen that look so many times while he played with my body that I found myself envying his guitar.

Tabitha swayed by my side. Every now and then, turning and smiling at me. She was happier than ever.

She screamed in my ear, "Isn't he hot? Isn't he sexy?" She'd also been bewitched by Thornhill magic. Of course, she was referring to Grant. And I had to admit, for a fifty-three-year-old, Aidan's dad cut a fine figure up there. He was as tall as his son, and he still managed a strong physique. His light-brown hair was long and graying, and with those entrancing blue eyes, I could understand Tabitha's attraction.

I wished I'd worn more suitable clothes, however. My green silk dress was a little dressy for the room. But it was impossible to resist Tabitha, who made me dance with her nonstop to the music. It was so much fun as we laughed like two crazy girls.

When a couple of guys joined us, I glanced up at Aidan. With his radar on high, as always, he cast a dark, penetrating frown at the men, followed by a sharp nod to Jack, his security guy, who'd been standing close. Dwarfing our eager wannabe dance partners, Jack signaled for them to leave us alone. The men shrank in defeat and left us to it. In her element, Tabitha looked at me and laughed.

After dancing through the whole set, Tabitha whisked me off to the restroom. I'd worked up a real sweat. It certainly beat going to a gym, something I'd avoided so far in my short life. I figured the daily rigorous workouts I got with my insatiable lover were sufficient to keep me in shape.

When I stared in the mirror, I winced. Before me was a mop of hair pathetically trying to be a bun, and eyeliner had smudged around my eyes. "Hmm... I look like I've been in a tornado." I giggled.

Tabitha grabbed her brush. "Here, let me do your hair."

My fatigued legs collapsed gratefully when I plonked onto a chair. After dancing forty minutes nonstop, and the deep, delicious straddling session with Aidan in the car, my body ached.

It was heavenly having Tabitha brush my hair. I closed my eyes and floated off. No pulls or pain. Her unflinching patience with my tangled mess of hair really did seem out of character for Tabitha, considering how restless she was. But when it came to hair and make-up, she approached it with the calmness of a Buddhist monk.

She lifted my heavy mane. "What do you want me to do with it?"

I dragged out an elastic band from my bag. "Here, a ponytail."

When she finished, I remained seated. My heavy body screamed for time out. It felt so nice to have a break. I watched Tabitha studying her flawless features closely in the mirror. She applied mascara to her long, thick eyelashes. After which, she dabbed natural lip-gloss onto her fleshy pout and fluffed her thick blond hair.

"You look beautiful, Tabs."

She gazed at me through the mirror. Her lips turned up at one end. "Thanks, sweetie. So do you. That dress is seriously sexy. Most of the guys have boners."

I scrunched my face "Gross."

She laughed before changing back to serious in a blink. "I'm soooo in love."

Hmm... I'd heard that before.

"I can see you guys are finding it hard to take your hands off each other. That's the second time I've seen you in a state of…"

"In a state of orgasmic delirium."

I laughed. "I suppose you can describe it that way. The first time was a little more confronting, seeing Grant's head buried between your legs."

Tabitha's eyes softened. "He's sexy. He licks me dry. And he is so fucking well-hung. I can barely walk afterward."

I recoiled. "Shit, Tabs, that's my future father-in-law you're talking about."

She placed her hands on her hips and huffed, "If I can't talk to you about my sex life, who else is there?"

I shrugged.

"You know me. Part of the fun is talking about it to my best friend." She put her arm around me and kissed my cheek. "I love you, Clary."

I kissed her back. "And I love you too, Tabs. It just feels weird. That's all."

"You'll get used to it. You're going to have to." She flashed one of those ambiguous smiles filled with a thousand meanings.

I was about to step outside when I turned. "What do you mean?"

Tabitha's lips curled up as her eyes danced with excitement. "He's asked me to marry him."

My eyebrows drew together sharply. "What? But you've only been together for two weeks."

She laughed. "I knew you'd say that." She looped her arm in mine. "Come on. Let's go and get our men before those older chicks in heat do."

I couldn't help but giggle as I followed my impulsive friend.

Aidan and Grant stood at the bar, talking to a couple of older women. Hmm… Tabitha was right. The cougars were circling. Aidan looked up and saw me. He bowed his head to excuse himself and approached me.

"Baby, there you are." He put his arm around my waist.

Like magnets, Grant and Tabitha were all over each other.

I stood on my toes and whispered, "Tabitha tells me they're getting married."

Aidan nodded slowly, looking nonplussed. "I know, Grant just told me."

"And you're cool about it?"

He shrugged. "What can I say? They're adults. Let them fuck up if they want to. Or it might work. Who knows? I know Dad's totally besotted."

"As is Tabitha." I peered up at Aidan. "I'm reading doubt in your words."

"She's not exactly reliable, is she? I mean, she was crazy about Evan a month ago."

I sighed. Aidan was right. I couldn't defend my erratic friend. I tilted my head and flashed a mock smile.

Aidan glanced over my shoulder. His face darkened. "Fuck. Speak of the devil." He lowered his voice. "Don't look now, but Evan's just turned up."

"What do we do?" I asked, fearing the worst.

"Leave it to me. I'll go and have a chat with him. I'll gauge his mood. Do me a favor, sneak Tabitha off to the bathroom. Stay there until I come and get you, okay?"

I nodded.

I headed over to get her but it was too late. Evan was standing by Tabitha. I could see alarm written on her face. He had her by the arm.

At first, there was no sign of Grant. Then, as I turned to look, I saw him racing toward the bar. He took Evan aside and said something. Evan's face had a brutal tightness about it as he shrugged violently out of Grant's hold.

They were locked in a war of words. Their faces nearly touching. Then Aidan stepped in and stood in the middle, separating them.

I watched with my heart in my mouth.

Luckily, Tabitha had the good sense to move away from them. She joined me, and I grabbed her by the hand. "Come on, quick. Let's go to the bathroom."

Her dampened hand trembled in mine as we moved along briskly. My instinct was to remain, however. I was frightened for Aidan. What if Evan had a knife? Or even a gun? My leaden legs made it difficult to walk.

When we entered the small room, I noticed there was no lock on the door, so I shuttled Tabitha, who was shivering, into a cubicle.

"Lock the door. And don't move. I'll be back in a minute. Promise me, Tabs."

"I will."

She was pale. I could see she was terrified, confirming the severity of Evan's threats. I'd never seen Tabitha that way. "Did he threaten to kill you?"

Her lips quivered as she broke down into tears. "He's got a gun."

My heart was now beating so hard I could hardly breathe. "Shit. Wait here."

When I left the restroom, I saw the three of them at the bar, talking. From where I stood, Evan seemed to have cooled down. I decided to call Aidan rather than approach them, and potentially inflame the situation, considering Tabitha's connection to me.

I sent him a text and observed as he reached for his phone and tapped something. It buzzed back.

It's under control. But don't come out. Wait for me there.

Ok. Aidan, be careful. He's got a gun.

I know. Don't worry. Just stay there.

I entered the restroom again. "Let me in, Tabs."

She opened the door, and I squashed into the tight cubicle, waiting for Aidan. We held hands in silence.

Five minutes later, I asked, "Are you okay?"

Tabitha shook her head. "I'm sorry. This is really fucked up. He threatened to kill me if I didn't go with him."

"How did he know you were here?"

"He found out I was seeing Grant," she said.

"How?"

"He ran into us on the street. Grant and I were walking arm in arm. All lovey-dovey." She raised a brow.

"Shit."

"Yeah. And I suppose he figured I'd be here with Grant."

"Did he tell you he had a gun?"

"Yep. He told me he'd use it on me and Grant if I didn't go out and talk to him."

My chest felt like stone. It was taking too long out there. I needed to know what they were doing.

A gunshot suddenly rang out, followed by screams.

Tabitha and I blanched. Her startled fear reflected the icy terror sweeping through my veins.

Tears filled my eyes. My heart squeezed into a tight ball. Was Aidan hurt? "Stay here," I urged, opening the cubicle.

Tabitha grabbed my arm. "No. Wait it out with me. There's nothing you can do."

The next moment, we heard yelling and another gunshot. I needed the toilet such was the visceral terror that had overtaken me. I pushed Tabitha off the seat, and a stream of anxiety cascaded down.

"What are we going to do?" I cried.

"Stay calm." Her trembling hand took my equally shaky hand.

The next thing I knew, the door swung open.

"Clarissa." It was Aidan, and I nearly collapsed from relief as I swung open the cubicle door.

I fell into his arms. "Aidan." He stroked my head. "It's okay, baby."

"We heard shots."

Tabitha was in his face. "Who was shot?"

Aidan looked pale.

My eyes enlarged. "Not Grant. Not your father?"

He shook his head.

Phew. I started to breathe again, and Tabitha sighed loudly.

"The police are coming now." He exhaled a long, jagged breath.

"Is anyone hurt?" I asked.

Aidan nodded. His eyes had gone dark.

"It's Evan, isn't it?" Tabitha asked.

"Yeah, he turned the gun on himself."

"But we heard two shots," I said.

Aidan rubbed his neck. "He aimed at Grant, but I managed to push the gun upwards. Luckily, it hit the ceiling. No one was hurt. Then Jack and Bob wrestled with him to get the weapon. Evan somehow managed to turn the gun inward and fired at himself." Aidan sighed roughly. His eyes were dark pools of sorrow. "That was his intention all along. He told me he had two bullets. One for Grant and one for himself."

I held Aidan tight. "I was so scared it was you, Aidan." Although I was relieved to be in his protective hold again, my universe had turned just as black as Aidan's mood, as I shriveled in his arms.

"We're safe, Angel. I need to be here for the cops. Then we'll go home, okay? Go into the band room. I'll get one of the guys to bring you a couple of drinks. I know I need one, desperately." He raked his fingers through his hair. "I'll join you as soon as I can." He kissed me. His mouth slightly quivery.

At least the band room was in the opposite direction, sparing us from witnessing the gruesome scene. Tabitha's mouth hung open on a blank, bloodless face, while we sat there speechless.

Grant entered and cast me an apologetic frown before taking Tabitha into his arms. Her body convulsed in sobs as he held her tight.

The realization hit me as I observed the touching scene in front of me. I could see plainly that Tabitha needed an older man to support her. Something told me that this relationship would stick. I recalled older, married Steve, whom she kept going back to. Although he was unavailable, Tabitha pined for him, even when she could have had any guy in her age group.

· · • ● · ● · · ·

I SAT SLUMPED ON the leather sofa. We'd decided to stay at Aidan's penthouse in Venice. What a night it had been. From scaling the heights of success after an auction that saw every painting sell—bringing in an excess of five hundred thousand for the VHC—to scraping the gloomy depths of despair.

Sitting with his head in his hands, Aidan was gutted.

I uttered, "I can't stop feeling responsible for what happened."

"You're not, Princess. Remove it from your thoughts. It's tragic enough as it is without you blaming yourself."

"But if I hadn't been around, Evan wouldn't have met Tabitha."

"Evan was a really disturbed guy."

I shook my head in disbelief. "Another one?"

He smiled grimly. "Yeah, I know. Everyone seems pretty fucked up. They were either before they entered the army, or after they left. Take your pick. In Evan's case, his problem started before. His mother was a whore and his father a pimp."

I grimaced. "Ouch."

He sniffed. "Yeah, that's how I reacted. He also admitted to me he got off on pushing women around."

"God, Aidan, why didn't you warn me?"

"Because I spoke to him when he hooked up with Tabitha and he assured me he was a new man. I'm sorry, I should've told you."

I took his hand and sat close. "You've got nothing to be sorry about. You looked after him. I mean, you employed him even after he'd admitted that to you. You did the best you could."

That night, we held each other tight. Aidan slept restlessly. He cried out, writhing about. It frightened me. I'd never seen him like that before. I didn't want to wake him because I didn't wish to shock him. I waited until his crying stopped, after which he fell into my arms. Pressed against his pounding heart, I eventually fell asleep.

The next morning, I woke and found Aidan on the pillow next to me, staring at me with a gentle smile.

"Hey," I said.

"Hey, Princess. You look so beautiful and peaceful when you sleep. You're bewitching even with those pretty eyes shut."

I brushed back my hair and lifted myself up.

"Don't get up. Stay here." He opened his strong arms. I fitted in perfectly. It was as if his strong body was made for mine. His biceps were cushiony and firm, better than any pillow, while his masculine scent sent a rush of heat through me.

"Aidan."

"Yes, Angel."

"You had a bad nightmare last night."

He turned his head sharply to face me. "What did I do?"

"You cried out and moved about."

"Did I hurt you?"

His eyes darkened with alarming intensity. Seeing that I'd touched a raw nerve, I shook my head emphatically. "I was more frightened for you."

He removed his arm from under my shoulder and sat up, combing back his hair, wearing a grim expression.

"What's wrong? It didn't worry me, really."

"I just don't recall. Normally, I do…" He spoke almost to himself.

"What do you mean by 'normally'?" I asked.

"I used to sleep roughly all the time before I met you. And even still, when I go away and sleep alone. The nightmares return."

"The shock of Evan, I'd imagine, Aidan." I stroked his cheek and snuggled close. "It didn't worry me. I was just upset for you. You seemed to be suffering."

"Nobody should have to experience that. I'm really sorry." He turned and brushed my face.

"Aidan, you could be possessed by the devil, and I still wouldn't leave you."

He laughed, releasing the tension that had blanketed our morning.

I snuggled up to him again. "In any case, the bed isn't just for sleeping, you know."

Aidan's eyes softened into a heart-melting turquoise shade. His lips curled up deliciously as he pulled back the covers. His eyes smoldering over my body left burning trails.

His hands caressed my breasts, making my body go steamy and tingly. Aidan's beautiful cock stood thick and hard. I licked my lips, but he got to them first, and our mouths met. Our frenzied tongues swirled together, tasting each other's need.

CHAPTER THREE

———◆◇◆———

AIDAN

TINY, COLORFUL FISH FLOATED behind the large tank, home to a miniature ecosystem. As always, the meditative scene gave me a much-needed break from the chaos ringing in my head.

Evan's death had unhinged me. An army of ghosts from my past had been unleashed, polluting my whole being with some fucked-up B-grade movie with no beginning or end.

Even Clarissa's gentle warmth, which normally calmed me, had done little to lift the dark curtain before me. Behind it, shadowy actors performed fractured sequences like film noir on acid. The script was my life before Clarissa. The actors, masked, deformed, and noisy, caused me, the director, to cry out in angst while I slept.

"Aidan." I looked up, and Kieren's placid smile put me at ease straight away.

"Thanks for seeing me on such short notice." I followed him into his office.

I sat on the comfy recliner he had in the corner, which was where I always sat. I refused to lie on the sofa. It was too clichéd and made me feel like a nut job.

"Can I offer you anything?" he asked, wiping his glasses.

I shook my head. "No, I'm good."

"What's been happening in your world?" he asked.

"A close buddy shot himself at the Red House. That's a music venue I own."

"I'm sorry to hear that. Suicide is frightful enough without having to witness it."

"You're not wrong there." I exhaled a long breath.

"I take it that this tragedy has triggered some dark memories."

"You could say that. My nightmares are back with a vengeance."

"That's no good. Tell me about them."

"Sometimes, I can't remember, to be honest. But Clarissa, who's with me every night, has told me I move about and cry out. One night, it was so bad she slept on the sofa." My voice trembled with the same frustration that had me wanting to punch a wall after discovering she wasn't by my side. "That's why I'm here, Kieren. I don't want this. I need her with me. Always. I sleep well with her there close. Peacefully. That was, until Evan…"

"This latest horror has opened up wounds, Aidan. It's understandable. Tell me, do you blame yourself for what happened?"

My jaw stiffened. "I do. It's because of me that he's dead."

"How could that be?"

"He fell in love with Clarissa's best friend, Tabitha. She then met my father and fell in love with him and left Evan. Evan was shattered. He'd called asking to see me that same day. I didn't find the time to catch up, only a short conversation on the phone. Perhaps if I'd gone and sat with him, he'd still be alive."

"That doesn't justify your guilt, Aidan. You spoke on the phone. What did he say?"

"He said that he was fucked up where women were involved and that he regretted treating Tabitha the way he did. He was into S&M. We'd already had a similar conversation a week earlier after I'd met him at a bar."

Kieren shifted in his seat. "I take it he was the aggressor?"

"Yeah. I don't get it, to be honest. I hate that sort of shit. Even though…" I rubbed my neck. Cold sweat trickled down my back. I reminded myself of my playful spanking sessions with Clarissa.

He sat forward. "Even though?"

"I sometimes play with Clarissa, you know? Roleplay. I don't hurt her, and she seems to enjoy it. It definitely excites me." I hated how inarticulate I sounded. "Am I fucked-up for doing that? Is that wrong?"

Kieren shook his head. "No. Roleplay is a natural outlet. It connects lovers to their childish, playful selves. There's no harm in it. The only harm is when it's non-consensual or when the submissive is coerced into acts that are painful, thereby inducing fear and dread. It's human nature to joke about. If anything, it's healthy for a relationship to be open and expressive."

My body relaxed into the cushions. "I believe Evan got pretty rough with Tabitha. She came to the estate with bruised arms and her back was marked."

"I'm not surprised she ran. She was being abused. Tell me, how was she in the beginning?"

"According to Clarissa, Tabitha described it as kinky and sexy. Clarissa was worried. I just kept out of it. You know, different strokes for different folks." I sniffed.

"Do you have any thoughts on why Evan shot himself publicly and not alone?"

I puffed up my cheeks and blew out slowly. "At the time he wanted to shoot my father. I was able to grab his hand in time and redirect the shot. My two security guys tried to get him to drop the gun. But somewhere in the middle of our pleading, he turned the gun and shot himself. It was a matter of seconds. I should have taken the gun. But Evan was a strong guy. I couldn't get it off him."

"This incident has obviously set off a flood of memories banked up in your subconscious."

"It seems so." I exhaled slowly. "It's crippling me. I should be tougher than this."

"No one has complete control of their buried thoughts. Put crudely, there are parts of our brain that house every fearful experience we carry. They soon form traumatic scars. By analyzing each fear and staring at it squarely in the eye, the intensity of that experience soon diminishes. Just like you're doing now, talking it through. Tell me, apart from Evan, are there other things happening in your life at the moment that are stirring you up?"

"Yeah, there are quite a few."

"Tell me about them."

"There's the Bryce Beaumont issue. You recall, he was blackmailing me about Ben?"

"Yes. He was threatening to report you."

"He's out on bail. He tried to kidnap Clarissa but failed when she fought him off." I couldn't help but smile, visualizing my angel kneeing Bryce in the balls.

"And is he still threatening? I mean, he's got the police watching him. That should be quietening him down, I imagine."

"To some extent. But he called me the other night, drunk and stoned. He told me he was writing a memoir that would implicate me."

"Can't your attorney do something about that? Sue him for slander?"

"I mentioned that. That doesn't freak me out. It's that he may harm Clarissa. But there's one other issue that's biting at me harder."

"Tell me."

"John Howard. He's the one that really worries me. He's out and free. I haven't heard or seen anything of him. But my mother, on a couple of occasions, mentioned he's out for blood. It's the hidden ones that frighten the most."

"Of course. Have you arranged surveillance on him?"

"Evan was doing that. He was the head of my security. It's all on file. I've got James, my other trusty security guy, on it now. Howard's being cased. But so far, nothing. He's keeping his distance."

"That's something, at least. Aidan, you must remember he's been locked up for thirteen odd years. I'm sure he doesn't really want to go back in. And were he to target you, it would lead the police straight back to him."

"Yeah, maybe." I held my head. I was tired. "Look, Kieren, you mentioned sleeping tablets. I don't like popping pills. But I don't want to chase Clarissa out of my bed, either. I need her there."

"I'll write you a script." He picked up a pad. "Evan sounds as if he had his own demons. I'm sorry you had to witness it, but I would say he would've done it anyway. Bryce is a weak man. Everyone knows that. By that, I mean your ex-commanding officers. I'm sure they'd find the words of a weak man hard to believe."

"I've already fessed up to my former senior officer, Kieren."

Kieren's eyes widened. "You have?"

I sighed. "I have. He just shrugged it off. As you know, there was no post-mortem on Ben. We couldn't get back to him. The area was surrounded by insurgents."

Kieren sat up. "What did he say exactly?"

"These were his words: 'War turns things upside down. Shit happens. You did the right thing. I would've done the same, considering that the Taliban would have dragged Ben's body through the streets like a trophy. If he had any breath left in him, that pain alone would've been unimaginable.'"

"Then you're exonerated, Aidan," he said.

I nodded. "I have to admit, it was a relief. I also told him about the cash. He just shrugged it off and reminded me that I'd furnished the widows' fund with twenty million dollars to date. He put his arm around me and told me that I was a model soldier who should have received a medal of valor, and that he was working on something to honor me for my philanthropic work. I told him that I didn't require a plaque or a medal for that. It was the least I could do to help. And left it at that."

"That negates Bryce's threats, then."

"It does. I'm just frightened he'll do something to harm Clarissa. That's my main fear. Not the Ben saga. Even if I had to do time for that, I would have gladly, you know. If I had to do it again, I'd do the same. I've made peace with Ben over that."

Kieren nodded pensively. "How so?"

I should have known Kieren wouldn't leave that comment alone. "One night recently, Ben visited me. He told me to stop carrying the weight of his death on my shoulders and to release the guilt. He was grateful and promised to protect me and Clarissa."

"Were you visited by nightmares again after that dream?"

"No. I was good. Even on my trips away. For a whole week, I slept like a baby. Then this thing with Evan happened, and now the ghosts are back."

"I see." He scribbled on a pad, then handed me the script.

I stood up and stretched my body. I took the script and stuffed it into my pocket. "Thanks, Kieren. I feel better."

"Good. Call me anytime." Kieren held out his hand and I took it.

As I left, I noticed a beautiful rose in his garden. It was stubborn, so I bent down and tore off the stem with my teeth while doing my utmost to avoid the thorns. The fragrance flushed hope through me, reminding me of beauty and Clarissa.

I called my favorite restaurant and booked a table, then called my beautiful girl.

As I stepped over the cracks in the pavement, a silly habit I'd adopted as a boy, I felt light for the first time in weeks.

CHAPTER FOUR

CLARISSA

IT NEVER CEASED TO amaze me how certain scents conjured up so many memories. The instant I stepped into Chris's studio a nostalgic muscle tweaked. Thick with linseed oil, paint fumes, and cigarette smoke, the heady mix took me back to my late mother's makeshift studio at home when I was young. It was a smell that I'd encountered all my life, probably even while I gestated in her womb because as I stood in Chris's studio, I was swept back to a time when I was a happy little girl playing with her paints.

Standing by my side, Aidan held my hand as Chris shuffled toward us, looking as scruffy as always. His eyes had that faraway glaze one got when lost in their own world.

As my attention turned to his latest creation—a larger-than-life depiction of Jessica—my veins iced, while Aidan stiffened by my side.

In the brilliantly crafted painting, she reclined in the nude with her legs slightly apart. Her eyes smoldered. I'd seen that same look directed at Aidan. She'd changed her hair shade to black—Hmm... funny about that. It sat provocatively over her voluptuous breasts, and her deep-red lips were slightly apart.

Noticing our stunned expressions, Chris said, "It's a commission. Jessica wanted it. And what Jessica wants, Jessica gets." He laughed, waiting for a response, but we remained mute. "I've gone all Egon Schiele but without the raw edges. To the line, I mean." He looked at me.

Aidan asked, "Egon Schiele?"

"He was a late nineteenth-century Austrian painter," Chris said, lighting a cigarette.

"He was known for his scandalous nudes," I added. "Only this is nothing like Schiele, in my opinion. His was a much cruder style."

"I don't know. It looks pretty damn crude to me," Aidan said, looking away.

Although I giggled, I still felt uncomfortable. I didn't like seeing Jessica so up close, pussy slit and all, in my face, confronting me. Mainly because it reminded me that Aidan had been there. I had the sudden urge to scratch out that smug expression, which Chris had masterfully captured.

"Sorry, guys. I should've covered it. Jessica's pretty wild. But she's a big payer." He stretched out his arm. "Come with me."

He led us to the other end of the studio and lifted the sheets off from six paintings. An "ah" escaped my lips when I saw myself in Aidan's arms on the chaise longue. I noticed Aidan's eyes glowing with appreciation. I could see he loved it as much as I did.

Chris, the master craftsman, had outdone himself.

"These are incredible," I said at last. He'd painted six varying versions of the same pose. Dressed in a green silk dress, I wore my hair down, and my diamond earrings sparkled brilliantly off the canvas. Aidan had his muscular arm around my waist.

But it was Aidan's handsome face that really made my heart pump. There was desire etched into his intense gaze. His eyes were such a luminescent blue my breath hitched. Both of our expressions reflected the love we shared. Chris had managed to show a seductive glint in Aidan's eyes—intense and playful at the same time. It was an expression only I thought I'd ever seen.

His commanding skill stole my breath. Even little things, like Aidan's enviable long lashes, were painted with such delicacy. I felt like touching them.

"My God, Chris, you've well and truly surpassed yourself with these," I said with breathy excitement.

Aidan squeezed my hand before releasing it so he could reach for his checkbook. "I want them all."

Chris's face lit up. Like most artists living on crumbs, he loved the smell of a sale.

After Aidan scribbled a one-hundred-thousand-dollar check that made Chris swoon, we left him alone, staring incredulously at the slip of paper.

Pinching my bottom after I stepped in front of him on the busy strip, Aidan gave me one of his irresistible grins. "Sexy butt. I love you in jeans, baby."

"Aidan, we're in public." I could see people checking us out and whispering.

He put his arm around me. "If a man can't touch his wife-to-be's butt, then there's something seriously wrong with the world."

"That canvas of Jessica was striking," I said. A twist of jealousy squirmed in my gut. I couldn't get over how gorgeous she looked.

"Mm... you think so?" Aidan drew me close to his waist.

"She's beautiful. And she wants you."

"Not for me, she ain't. Jessica's fake, darling. Every square inch. Not like you." He rubbed my butt again. "This peachy, chubby little butt. Mm... I love rubbing myself against you."

My eyebrows drew in sharply. "Chubby?"

Aidan laughed. "Oh, baby. It's not chubby in an ugly way. But in a super sexy, curvy way."

I turned to look at him. He was aroused. My insecurity made me wonder if seeing Jessica naked had done that to him. I looked down. Oh my, he had a bulge.

"It was pretty sexual."

"What was, baby?" Aidan opened the car door and helped me up into the SUV.

"Jessica," I said with a cranky edge.

"Not for me, it wasn't."

After Aidan settled into his seat, he turned to look at my sullen face. "Hey, what's up?"

"I feel so insecure. She's so sophisticated. I'm just a bumbling little girl who... I don't know."

Aidan leaned over and took me into his arms. "Hey, Clarissa. You're my life. No one compares to you, sweetheart. You're beautiful, intelligent, and sexy as hell."

"But I'm shy."

"That's sexy in my book. Come on, let's go home. If you keep going on about how unsexy you are, I'm going to have to spank you." He raised an eyebrow. His lips curled up deliciously.

My veins thawed. Aidan's smiling gaze was as irresistible as usual, making me giggle. I slapped his muscular thigh. "You're incorrigible, Aidan."

"Around you, I am." He pressed a button and the Doors came on. He sang along in that arousing pitch-perfect rasp, as we headed back to paradise.

The next morning, I went to the cottage to visit Tabitha. I'd called beforehand to make sure I didn't turn up when she was with Grant. By that stage, I was convinced that my future father-in-law was as addicted to sex as my best friend.

I found Tabitha on the porch with her bare feet up on the table, drinking coffee.

"Hey you," she said, all smiles and looking as gorgeous as ever, her hair down and golden, her eyes wide and bright. Tabitha was one of those rare species who could go with little sleep and still look stunning.

"You're in a good mood."

"I should be. Grant's asked me to move in."

"When?"

"Tomorrow."

I frowned. "That soon? I'll miss you. I liked having you here."

"I've loved being here, too. It's like stepping into a twilight zone. Everything's so yesterday—in a pretty way, that is." She chuckled.

"I love it here that much, I never want to leave," I said.

"It suits you, Vintage Girl." She smiled. "So what should we do on our last day together?"

"Aidan left this morning for New York. He asked me to go to an estate auction on Sunset Boulevard. An old Hollywood producer with a penchant for Art Deco has passed away. Aidan wants some of those lovely dancer figurines, lamps, and colored glass vases, which I simply adore. He asked me to go and buy as much as I want. Apparently, there are silk dresses from the twenties and thirties," I gushed. "When I heard that, I jumped. I might even be able to pick up a dress for my wedding."

Tabitha's head pulled back sharply. "A wedding dress? Clary, you're not going all vintage on me again, are you? I thought we could design one together. I was looking forward to that."

"Let's see what's there. I must admit, the thought of one of those slinky satin numbers like Greta Garbo wore sends shivers of excitement through me."

"It will also send shivers through the male guests." Tabitha stretched her arms. "Garbo was svelte and almost flat-chested, sweetie. With your curves and boobs, it may leave the celebrant gasping for air."

I laughed. "I'll make sure that I tape down my breasts and wear a bra with lots of support. Do you want to come along?"

"Yeah. You bet. Sunset Boulevard. Let's do lunch at the strip, first. We can rub shoulders with the rich and filthy."

"You mean filthy rich," I said.

"No, I mean rich and filthy."

I smiled. I loved having Tabitha to share in my adventures. "Let's do that."

James, my driver, was meant to take us. Aidan even reminded me after he'd caught me driving to the VHC. But with Tabitha in tow, I felt like being independent.

After finally managing to park the car, we entered the busy street, which was predictably filled with hordes of strange entities. Some didn't even look like people, and going by the glazed looks on their faces, I got the impression that they hadn't slept for a long time. Every day was the morning after, on that strip. As we pranced along, it felt as if we'd landed on another planet.

The novelty soon wore off after being continually refused entry into many of the cafes. Like all the establishments we'd already tried, the waiter looked us up and down and shook his head. "Sorry, ladies. We don't have any tables available."

Leaning into my ear, Tabitha muttered that we should've worn designer. I couldn't believe it, given that there were empty tables everywhere.

Tabitha bristled at one of the waiters while pointing at me. "You do realize this is Aidan Thornhill's future wife?"

I elbowed Tabitha and shook my head ever so slightly. Nevertheless, as wilful as always, she persisted. "We can call Aidan if you like and ask him to vouch for us."

As much as I resented airing my private credentials, it worked. His mien softened at the mention of Aidan's name. "Let me see. Inside or out?"

"Outside, please," said Tabitha.

He pointed to a table on the promenade. I imagined it was a coveted position because one could watch the endless parade. "Alfredo will direct you ladies to table eight," he said.

Tabitha stood behind him, puffing her cheeks and crossing her eyes. Her childish prank forced me to squeeze my lips tight. I bowed my head in gratitude. I was too scared I would explode in laughter otherwise.

As we followed the waiter, I elbowed Tabitha, who responded with an "ouch."

"I wish you wouldn't do that," I whispered.

In typical rebellious form, she continued playing up by mimicking the waiter's girlish walk.

That did it. I lost all self-control and laughed, fueled by Tabitha's squealing giggles. The waiter stared at us. I felt bad, hoping he wouldn't think we were laughing at him. In reality, we were probably laughing more at how ridiculous the whole situation was. And how unreal everyone seemed.

Tabitha said, "Sorry, we had a big night." She raised an eyebrow.

He returned a knowing little smile before taking our orders.

We both ordered lasagna, salad, wine for Tabitha, and mineral water for me.

"You should have used your driver. We could have shared a few wines together and made a day of it," she said.

"Drinking wine during the day puts me to sleep. I don't know how you manage it."

"Irish genes, sweetie." She lounged back with a self-satisfied grin.

We attracted more attention than I liked. I hated how the patrons glared at us. I supposed we looked like two ordinary girls sitting at a prized table. Tabitha had made more of an effort with her low-slung jeans and loose, ruffled pink blouse, whereas I'd chosen a vintage cotton floral shift and green cardigan.

I leaned in. "Everyone's staring for some reason."

She pointed at my outfit. "Maybe that grandma dress has got something to do with it."

"I love this dress."

"So, you always say. And you're not wearing a stitch of makeup. That's considered weird around here."

I did a quick survey of all the patrons and noticed how made up everyone was. Even some of the men had foundation on. I supposed most were probably actors. I did recognize a few faces.

"Ah… here we go," she said, looking over my shoulder.

A couple of guys strutted over to join us. They were like weightlifters, and their tanned, oily muscles glistened in the sun.

"Hey, girls. Mind if we join you?" Their smiling eyes glowed with confidence.

Tabitha looked them up and down. "Yes."

He went to sit down. My eyes widened, pleading for Tabitha to use that smart mouth of hers to stop him. Sure enough, she looked at Mr. Muscles and said, "That was a no."

"How about after lunch, we get together?" His tanned features cracked into a confected smile.

Tabitha shook her head.

I was glad when the waiter arrived with our drinks. My expression must have been signaling for help because the waiter whispered, "Are these men disturbing you, ma'am?"

I nodded.

He mumbled something to one of them, who then shuffled off, but not before sneering at us.

"What a douche," Tabitha said. "He can barely move he's so muscle-bound."

I nodded. "He walks like a bear."

As we sat there, enjoying our delicious lunch, we were entertained by the panoply of strange beings swanning and strutting by. From women wiggling along in very tight, skimpy gear, some with butts that poked out so much, Tabitha and I conjectured they were padded.

There were tattooed men everywhere. Lots of beards, and older, tanned men that I was sure were at least thirty years older than their stunned faces suggested. There were men that were women and women that were men.

"I haven't had this much fun in ages," Tabitha said.

"Yeah, it beats going to the circus," I said.

CHAPTER FIVE

AFTER LUNCH, WE HEADED for the auction. Even though it was due to commence at three in the afternoon, I needed time to view the items properly and closely. Everything was up for sale, and since it was a large mansion, we were in for a long day.

When we pulled up at the impressive pre-war mansion, Tabitha whistled. "Do you think we'll be greeted by Norma Desmond?"

I chuckled at Tabitha's reference to the fading starlet from the 1950s film *Sunset Boulevard*.

"I don't know. But I'd love to run into a William Holden look-alike."

"Oh... yeah," crooned Tabitha.

I pressed the buzzer and explained who I was. The gates opened, and we drove up the snaky driveway.

After I managed to find a place to park, a security guard came to meet us.

"Follow me," he said.

The grounds were magnificent—ancient willows amongst flourishing bushes, statues of goddesses, and birdbaths. It had that same old-world charm as Aidan's beautiful estate.

As we paced the path my body rang with anticipation at what delightful goodies awaited us inside. I could never have imagined that this would become my life, being able to buy all that my heart desired. It was so strange that at times it felt as if I were living in a dream.

When we stepped through the French doors, my eyes fell upon a collection of prints.

"Oh..." I sighed loudly, as I studied the frames of draped women embedded in a celebration of swirls. "Alphonse Mucha."

"They're pretty," said Tabitha.

"They're not just pretty, they're sensational posters from the Art Nouveau era."

A couple of men joined us. They were about our age and good looking in that super-confident-rich-boy-way.

"My mother was rather fond of those," said one of the men. Due to his gym gear, I figured he belonged to the house.

"Hi. I'm Nathan, and this is Jason." He pointed to his friend, who was also in gym gear.

In a flirtatious mood, as always, Tabitha flashed an encouraging smile. I held out my hand. "Pleased to meet you. I'm Clarissa, and this is Tabitha."

"You've come for my auction, I take it?" Nathan asked. His lips formed a slight curl after he ran his eyes up and down my outfit.

As always, I looked out of place in my 1960s textured, black-and-green-polka-dot dress. But then something told me that it didn't matter what I wore as long as I had a checkbook in my bag. I could've turned up in my pajamas, and they'd still serve me champagne. Money did that to people. The richer you were, the more eccentric you could be.

"Are these"—I pointed at the Mucha frames—"up for sale, as well?"

He nodded. "Sure are. Everything is. It's all mine now. And even though I appreciate beauty"—his warm green eyes rested on my face—"I'm more into contemporary designs."

Jason, meanwhile, had cornered Tabitha. I heard him whisper something about a casting call. *Probably more a casting couch.*

We were off to a good start. Two seriously overconfident dudes hitting on us.

As I watched the rest of the potential buyers entering, I could see that we stood out as odd for that type of event. Nathan probably thought we were interlopers. There to see how the rich lived, in the hope of meeting rich young men.

I decided to call Aidan to ask about buying the Muchas. I imagined they would look gorgeous with those gilded frames on the red wall in the dining area.

Tabitha, meanwhile, chatted with Jason while Nathan hung close at my heels like an eager puppy dog.

I stepped away from the trio and grabbed my phone out of my bag. I pressed on Aidan's handsome face.

He picked up straight away. "Hey, Princess."

"I hope I'm not disturbing you," I said.

"Never. How's the auction?"

"That's why I'm calling. I know you sent me on a mission for objet d'art and I'm getting around to looking at those, but I've stumbled on six framed Muchas. They're Art Nouveau posters of neo-classical women. They're just exquisite. I can send you a couple of images if you like. I thought they'd look lovely in the dining room."

"Baby, buy whatever your heart desires. I've just spent all morning going over my finances and discovered I made a billion dollars in the past week. The pie just keeps growing. We're ridiculously rich, Angel."

"You're ridiculously rich," I said with a chuckle.

"What's mine is yours, Clarissa. And baby..."

"Yes?"

"I love you."

My heart melted. "I love you, too, Aidan."

"Bye, sweetheart."

"Bye." I put my phone away in my bag.

I floated on a dreamy cloud, all warm and fuzzy, when Nathan approached me and asked, "Can I offer you a drink?"

I glanced over at Tabitha. Jason held a bottle of champagne in the air, ready to fill her glass.

"No, I'm good. I'm driving."

He nodded. His sparkling eyes lingered, and suddenly I found myself conjuring up ways of giving him the brush-off without seeming rude.

"I best keep moving. I'm pretty keen to see everything before the auction starts."

"I can show you around. If there's anything you really like, I'm happy to negotiate a price so that you don't have to wait for the hammer to go down." He raised his eyebrows with an eager smile.

"Now that you mention that, I would like the six Muchas."

He cocked his head. "You're aiming high. They're the big-ticket item."

"I'm not surprised. I still want them," I said matter-of-factly.

"I'll have to have a chat with my advisor on those."

"I'm happy to bid for them like everyone if need be." I looked over at Tabitha, who was laughing and joking with Jason. I hoped she wasn't about to cheat on Grant. That friend of mine was in heat and out of control.

When I finally caught Tabitha's eye, I crooked my finger.

"What?" she asked.

"I hope you're not leading him on."

"No. He's a producer. He wants me to go in for a screen test. Can you believe it?"

"Yeah, of course, I believe it. I've been trying to get you to Hollywood for years. You're a natural, Tabs. Just don't fuck him."

She saluted with two fingers on her forehead. "Yes, Mom."

"Are you coming?"

"Lead the way." She looped her arm around mine and cast Jason a little smile, encouraging him to follow. "I think they like us, Clary," she whispered.

"They can stare, but not touch."

Figurines of women in tulip-shaped gowns, upper bodies arched and heads fallen back, stole my breath. I was in heaven. Nathan's late father certainly loved Art Deco. There were so many, I was like a child in a candy store. My "wows" bounced off the walls with each artifact. It was not going to be easy, considering there were three rooms of objects to look at.

By the end of it, I was exhausted and indecisive. I wanted them all.

Nathan approached me. "I've spoken to Brendan. The frames are yours for fifty thousand dollars. We were going to start the bidding at forty thousand."

I stretched out my hand. "It's a deal. I'll take them."

He regarded me for a moment, nodding slowly. "Good. I'll instruct my man to put a sold sticker on them."

"I'm sure I'll be making other purchases today. If you like, I can write one check for everything together."

"Whatever's easier for you." He paused to study me. "Do you live around here?"

Tabitha answered for me. "No, she's a Malibu girl."

"Nice." He glanced at Tabitha then looked back at me. "When all this is over, do you feel like having a drink or dinner later on tonight, maybe?"

I smiled. "That's sweet. Only, I should tell you that I'm engaged."

His eyes went down to my finger where the outrageously big diamond sat. I was surprised he hadn't noticed it.

"Wow. Look at that. Still, I don't mind if you don't mind." He flashed a large smile.

"No, I'm good. Thanks." I left him there and continued on. Tabitha flanked me. "He just asked me out. I can't believe he didn't notice my ring," I whispered.

"He's been too occupied with your eyes, and exploding bosom, I think," she said dryly.

I giggled. "Let's go and check out the gowns. I'm dying to see them. Come on. Hurry. We don't have much time. I may need to try one on."

Tabitha skipped along. The mention of clothes always put a spring in her step.

There were two racks of long, silk dresses. Being from the thirties, they were mainly in shades of champagne, antique pinks, and moony creams. They were so deliciously satin that as our hands glided down the silky fabric. We "aahed" in chorus.

"Oh my, God." Tabitha took one off its hanger. The streamlined tulip design promised to flatter the body by hugging to the thighs before flouncing out. It was creamy, rich silk satin with diamantes around the neckline, on the straps, and low-cut back.

"This is sexy as hell," she purred, running her hands over the fabric.

I held it up. "It's gorgeous. Do you think it's appropriate for a wedding dress?"

She held it against my body. "It sure is."

"It looks as if it would fit."

"Quick, try it on," said Tabitha.

I stepped out from behind the oriental screen and twirled. As expected, the dress flared out, floating in the air gracefully. It felt smooth and slippery against my skin and as I stood before the mirror, the sensuous gown caused my temperature to rise as I imagined Aidan's fingers sliding over it.

"Clary, it looks amazing."

Tilting my head from side to side, I had to agree. I played with the flouncing neckline. "I'm hanging out a fair bit." The spaghetti straps meant that I had no support whatsoever. "I'm going to have to strap my breasts down with something, and with this low-cut back, I'm not sure how I'll do that." I turned and studied how the gown hugged my curves like a glove.

"It's as if it were made for you. It's fucking gorgeous," Tabitha enthused. "We'll figure out what to do with those boobs of yours. It's so you. You've got to wear it." She rummaged through a chest and brought out a piece of cream lace. She placed it on my head so that it cascaded over my shoulders.

"Freaking hell. Will you look at that? We have a perfect match."

Tabitha was right. The lace, which appeared handmade, was elaborately florid and ideally suited to the simplicity of the dress.

Tears filled my eyes. I couldn't believe how quickly we came to it. It was a piece of magic at work. "Shit, Tabs, it shouldn't be this easy, should it?"

She held her chin and shook her head. Her eyes were aglow. "You look gorgeous. It's a must."

After I returned to my former self, I went searching for Nathan. I couldn't risk losing the dress at auction. I had to have it.

As soon as I entered the room, Nathan, who had been chatting with prospective buyers, gazed up at me.

"Can I have a quick word?" I asked.

"Sure thing," he said, all smiles and hanging close.

"I want to buy this dress and lace." I lifted my arms, holding the cascading slinky dress.

He raised an eyebrow. "Only if you let me see you in it."

I frowned. "Are you joking?"

He shook his head. "No." He was serious.

Shit.

I went over to Tabitha. "He won't sell me the dress unless I model it for him."

Tabitha laughed. "Boy, he's keen."

"What do I do?"

"Do you want the dress?"

I nodded.

She shrugged. "That's your answer."

Nathan waited patiently while I went back behind the screen. It felt weird and wrong, but I had to have that dress.

When I stepped out, I saw his face change color. Even though I'd kept my bra on, my nipples poked through the flimsy fabric. He noticed because his eyes darkened with arousal. He pointed. "Turn around."

I reluctantly moved.

"It looks absolutely stunning. You're beautiful, Clarissa," he said. Approaching me, he brushed my shoulder. His eyes glanced down at my cleavage.

I crossed my arms and looked down at my feet. "Is that enough? Can I take it off?"

He nodded. "Sure. The dress is yours. Thank you. It fits you beautifully. It was made for you. Keep it."

"I want to pay for it," I said as he was about to leave the room.

"It's yours," he said.

I went to my handbag and pulled out my checkbook. "I have to pay for it."

He shrugged. "You just bought those frames. That was a tidy sum. And I'm sure you're about to shell out at the auction. Take this as a gift."

"But I want to pay." I scribbled ten thousand on the check and handed it to him. Nathan's head pulled back sharply.

"That's generous. Look, that's a night out for me. Keep it, really."

"I need you to take it. The dress is for my wedding."

His eyes widened with surprise. "Nice one. He's a lucky man. Tell you what. Go in there"—he pointed to another room— "and take whatever you fancy. Then we have a deal, okay?"

I shrugged. He was adamant and I really wanted the dress. I nudged Tabitha, who was bantering and giggling with Jason.

When we were out of earshot, I said, "Tabs, you're leading him on."

"Hmm... and loving it."

"But what about Grant? You better not fuck around with him, Tabs."

"Hey... chill. We were just arranging for me to do a screen test."

"Let's hope he hasn't got a nice big comfy sofa in his office," I said sarcastically.

"You're such a grandma, Clary, especially in that cardigan and that 1950s attitude."

"What's that supposed to mean?" I asked with my hands on my hips.

"Nothing." She linked her arm with mine.

The Art Deco figurines did not disappoint. There were too many to choose from—women with bendy backs, in arabesque poses, and gowns splayed out as they twirled. There were also antique Murano glass vases that I just couldn't resist. Some items, I purchased as homecoming gifts for my father and Greta. I also bought a pair of matching figurine lamps for Tabitha.

CHAPTER SIX

—◆◇◆—

IT WAS GETTING DARK when we drove off. I was hungry and exhausted, so we stopped for a cheeseburger and shake before taking the trip home. Tabitha had arranged to meet Grant at his house, but I got her to change it for the estate after I begged her to come back with me.

I was there alone and really needed someone I could talk to if need be. Susana, I barely spoke to. Will was there, but since he was Susana's lover, I found conversation with him lacking. Roland, his son, was out most nights, and Linus, our security guy, hung out in his cottage, which was situated quite a distance from the main house. It was strange being in such a big estate alone. I couldn't wait for my father and Greta to return.

Aidan had offered for me to go to New York with him. But with the auction happening, I'd decided to stay. In any case, he was due back the following day. I couldn't wait. I missed him badly.

After polishing off our burgers, we took off for Malibu. As we drove along the windy coastal highway, I could see the sea swallowing the sun. The fiery ball sank, leaving behind a delicate bleeding turquoise sky, delightfully surprising, as always.

Tabitha sang along to Beyoncé on the radio, while my mood was heightened following an afternoon of staring at beautiful objects. My wedding dress on the backseat, the prize. Tingles of anticipation rippled through me. My wedding day had suddenly materialized in the shape of a seductive wedding gown. I couldn't wait to see Aidan's aquamarine gaze as I walked down the aisle.

A car with blinding lights suddenly appeared behind me. It was really close. Too close for comfort. The vehicle's lights were so blinding, I couldn't stare for long in the rearview mirror.

"Freaking hell, that car is really close," I said.

Tabitha looked over her shoulder. "Fuck," she uttered. Her dramatic tone pretty much summed up the sudden tightness in my chest.

I stepped on the accelerator, but it continued to tail me. "Shit, Tabs it's close to ramming us."

"Just keep an eye on the road. You're doing fine."

I was already breaking the speed limit. The curvy coastal road didn't leave much room for error either.

"Should I pull off somewhere?" I asked.

Tabitha had her head turned, focusing on the vehicle behind us. "Fuck, that's one determined sonofabitch."

I couldn't help checking the rearview mirror. If I slowed down, the large SUV would knock our little car off the road. I regretted not driving Aidan's SUV. More importantly, I regretted not having James drive us.

I'd forgotten to breathe. My mouth was dry and bitter tasting.

There was a turnoff. I took it sharply.

Tabitha let out a cry. "Whoa. Good one." She turned to check behind us. "We've lost him."

I decided to pull up in a driveway that was surrounded by trees in order to hide.

As we sat there, I asked, "What should I do now?"

"Let's wait for a few minutes. Are there any other routes back to the house?"

"No," I said.

Ten minutes passed. Tabitha hadn't uttered a word, confirming she was just as frightened as I was.

I started the car. My hands clutched the steering wheel tightly. I had to remind myself to breathe as I turned back toward the highway.

Tabitha looked behind us at the same time as me.

"It's clear. Quick, let's get back."

I put my foot down on the accelerator and got up to the acceptable speed. Finding my composure, at last, I turned on the radio.

Before long, the lights reflected off my side mirror again. I glanced into the rearview mirror and, sure enough, the SUV was back on our tail.

"Shit. He's back."

Tabitha turned sharply. "Holy fuck. This dude's determined."

"Yeah, too much so. Call 911, quick. There's something wrong."

She pressed the button and spoke. "We're on the Pacific Coast Highway, heading for Malibu. A car is trying to ram us. Yeah, that's right. He's been following us for a while. Please hurry." She turned and looked. "There doesn't appear to be a license plate. Yes, I'll hold."

I turned to look at her briefly. I had one eye on the rearview mirror and one eye on the road. "What's happening?" I asked.

"Watch the curve!" Tabitha yelled.

I swerved and nearly hit a car heading in the opposite direction.

"Okay, sure," Tabitha said. "Please tell them to hurry."

The vehicle bumped us, and we screamed. "Shit, Clary. Step on it."

I did just that. My eyes were on the road ahead. I had to keep stopping myself from looking in the mirror. My heart was beating so fast I was frightened I was going to have a heart attack.

It bumped us again.

My senses heightened. Adrenaline charged through my veins. Instead of fear, I suddenly felt angry. In my mind, images flashed of Aidan holding me tight.

I had to survive, if only just to feel my true love again. No one was going to take that away from me, I thought. As raging blood pumped through me, I went into battle.

There was no vehicle coming toward us. It was then or never, I told myself. Biting my lip, I performed a decisive U-turn. It was sharp. It needed to be. There was little room for error. The wheels squealed, and the car swerved, scraping the barrier. Fortunately, it aligned itself, thanks to the brilliant stabilizing mechanisms embedded in the nimble vehicle. At least that was one of the advantages of driving a small car.

Tabitha held her mouth. Although it was a matter of seconds, time stretched, and every little moment, one frame at a time, stood out sharply.

"Holy fuck!" cried Tabitha.

We heard a deafening screech of tires, and as I looked in the mirror, I saw that our determined enemy had pulled the same stunt. His heavy vehicle swung around. Only, as it swerved, the heavy bull-bar in the front knocked down the barrier and the vehicle tumbled down the cliff face.

"Oh my God!" Tabitha cried out.

I slowed down. A vehicle was behind me. Therefore, I couldn't stop.

Luckily, in only a matter of seconds, a parking lot appeared at the side of the road. I pulled up there.

Finally, I was able to breathe again. My body was drenched in cold sweat. I noticed that the charge in the electric car was down. There was no way we'd get back home with that little power. Still, the brilliant mechanics of the vehicle had saved our lives.

Tabitha and I looked at each other and shook our heads in disbelief. She was as white as a ghost.

"What do we do now?" I asked.

I looked ahead and saw the police with their lights flashing, heading toward us. I jumped out of the car and waved them down.

Tabitha's phone buzzed. She picked up, uttered, "Grant" and started to cry.

I ran to the policemen. Tears flooded down my face. The adrenaline that had saved us had been replaced by deep sobs.

My mouth opened, but the words were stuck in my throat.

"You called us, ma'am," said one of the policemen, writing down the license plate number.

I pointed down the precipice. "There's been an accident. Farther back about... not far, a few hundred feet or so. I think." My voice was breathless.

"Have you called 911?"

I shook my head and cried.

"It's okay. It just happened, I take it?"

I nodded.

He spoke into his phone and gave directions while his colleague stood on the side of the road, flashing a light down the cliff face.

The colleague ran back to him. "I spotted something. I'll go and check it out."

The policeman nodded and returned to me. "We got the distress call saying that you were rammed by that vehicle. Is that right?"

Cradling my body, I nodded. It wasn't a cold night, but my teeth chattered while my sweaty body trembled.

"Are you okay for me to take a statement now? Is there anyone you can call to come and help you? You've got a friend with you, I see."

We glanced over at Tabitha, who was still on the phone with Grant. When the policeman nodded toward her, she ended the call and joined us.

"Boy, are we glad to see you," said Tabitha. "It was seriously scary. They were trying to kill us."

"I'm told that you were being pursued by the SUV and that it knocked into your vehicle?"

Tabitha nodded. The policeman walked around to the back of the car and shone his flashlight on the car. "I can see indentations here. Have you got someone who can come and get you?" he asked, looking at me.

"Yes. James, my driver."

Noting his eyebrow rising, Tabitha blurted, "Clarissa is Aidan Thornhill's fiancée."

"I see. He's been informed of this?"

I bit my lip. "Not yet." My voice was small.

"Well then, we need to impound this vehicle for our investigation. I'll wait here with you for your driver."

The ambulance came screaming toward us. I looked at the policeman. "Can you tell us what happened to the driver? I mean…" Tears ran down my eyes. Was he dead?

"All in good time. For now, make that call."

My phone buzzed. It was Aidan. I looked up at the policeman. "Do you mind if I take this? It's my fiancée."

The policeman nodded and then headed off to the ambulance, which had pulled up behind my car.

"Aidan." The sob was deep in my throat. My voice was thick. I was doing my utmost not cry.

"What's happened? Grant rang me and told me that you've been in an accident. Are you okay?" The desperation in his tone only added to my anguish.

"I'm fine, Aidan. It's a long story. The police are here. The car that was chasing us has rolled down the embankment. I don't know if he's alive or dead." My voice broke into a sob.

"What car?"

"I don't know, Aidan. We were driving along when it started to push us along."

"Who was driving, Clarissa. James?"

I took a deep breath. My nails dug into my palm. "No, I was." My voice was so small. I was sure I did it on purpose so he wouldn't hear my answer.

"Where's James?" Aidan's voice went up a decibel. I felt the tremor in his tone. I could tell Aidan wanted to erupt but was trying to control it. "Clarissa, you were meant to be with him."

"Please don't, Aidan. Not now. I just want to go home."

I heard a jagged breath in my ear. "Yeah, sure. It's just that... fuck, Clarissa." He paused to breathe out his frustration. "You're not hurt are you, baby?"

"I'm okay. I just want to go home." My voice drowned in tears.

"You're safe now, princess. Don't worry. I'll call James now. He can track you. I'm on my way home as we speak. I should be there in two hours."

"I need you, Aidan. This has been..." I broke down again. "I'm sorry."

"Hey, don't be sorry. I'll get off now so I can call James, okay? See you soon, Clarissa. I love you."

"I love you too." I sniffled.

Tabitha and I piled into James's SUV. I'd never felt happier to see my driver than at that moment. We sat quietly in the backseat, holding onto each other for the whole ten-minute journey.

When we finally arrived, I stepped out of the car. "Thanks, James. I'm sorry I didn't get you to drive me around."

His smiling dark, gentle eyes reflected understanding. "Hey, it's cool. I'm just glad you're okay."

Tabitha and I walked along the cobbled path. Normally, I'd amble along and enjoy the aesthetics of the garden at night with the lamps lighting up the trees and casting sculptural shadows everywhere. But at that moment, all I wanted was a stiff drink and a bath.

Grant was in the middle of a show and on his break when he'd called. He promised to come straight over afterward to be with Tabitha.

I left her at the cottage. "Are you going to be okay until Grant gets here?"

"Yeah." We hugged each other again. "I'm going to soak in a bath with a crisp white." She smiled gently. This was not my bombastic friend. This was an earnest version that pretty much reflected my state— a mixture of relief, fear, and exhaustion.

"Hey, do you think he's still alive?" I asked.

Tabitha's mouth turned down. "Don't know. Whatever happened, the fucker deserved it. He wanted to kill us, Clary."

My face pinched. "But why?"

"Has Aidan got many enemies?"

"A few, I think," I answered, sighing. Bryce's greasy, desperate face came to mind. I grabbed my arms and shivered. "I need to go up, Tabs. Are you sure you'll be okay here?"

"I'll lock the door. Grant should be here in about an hour."

When I entered the dining area, I was relieved to find it empty of Susana. She was the last person I wanted to lay eyes on. I didn't want her to see a broken version of me, for some reason.

My heavy body barely made it up the stairs. I opened the door to the large room and turned the lamps on before heading for the bathroom.

I stood in the Moroccan-tiled bathroom, big enough to house a small family, and went over to the large sunken bath to turn on the taps. As the water gushed out I stripped off my clothes.

I lowered my shaky frame onto the smooth floor of the tub and exhaled deeply as the warm water cascaded over my shivering skin. Leaning my neck back into the indented padding, I finally released the tightness in my body.

Twisted faces and dark clouds left my thoughts. I had finally managed to unwind when Aidan entered.

I looked up. He was unshaven, his hair tousled, and his face wore a haunted, lost expression. Aidan's eyes were so darkly serious, my body tightened again. I read self-blame in that gorgeous, but broken face.

Not one word was uttered. He just stripped out of his clothes and jumped into the bath with me. He sat behind me and wrapped his arms around me. Tears pooled in my eyes. The anguish I'd been carrying suddenly melted away in his strong arms.

We remained like that for a long while, holding each other. It was as if we were waiting for the warm water to wash away the tension that had swallowed our blissful lives.

It wasn't until I was on the sofa, dressed in a thick bathrobe, with a whiskey in hand, that I found my voice.

"Clarissa, why didn't you use James?"

I resented his annoyed tone. "Aren't you just pleased I got out of it alive?"

He combed his hair back with his fingers, pacing about like a tiger looking for a victim. "I am. But you've got to follow orders. They're there for a good reason."

"And what's that?" My voice had a touch of ice. "That you have a ton of enemies that want to harm us?"

An uneven breath left his parted lips. "I'm sorry, Clarissa, for dragging you into my fucked-up world. It's the last thing I want for us." He poured himself some bourbon and gulped it down.

"I just wanted to have a day out with Tabitha. You know? A normal day. Have lunch, then off to the auction." I thought about the dress in the backseat of the car that the police had taken away. My brow puckered in despair.

He shook his head. "What?"

"I found an exquisite dress to wear for our..." I burst out crying. This was the first time we'd been heated with each other. It wasn't my thing, this defensive stance. But Aidan's authoritative attitude had stiffened my back.

"For our wedding?" he asked. Aidan's eyes softened, and he came to me and took me into his arms. "Baby, I'm sorry. I shouldn't have gotten angry with you. It's just that if anything had happened to you..."

My body liquefied in his strong arms. "Do you think I'll get my dress back?"

Aidan's tightened expression softened. He brushed my cheek. "I'll make sure of it."

"Promise me you won't look at it."

Aidan's lips curled for the first time since arriving. He held his finger up. "Scout's honor."

We exchanged a gentle smile and held each other tight.

· · ● · ● · ● · ● · ·

THE FOLLOWING MORNING, AIDAN took a call from the police while I ate my breakfast out on the balcony.

I knew that I'd have to go in and make more statements. I was obsessing over my dress so much that I'd forgotten to think about anything else. It was probably a distraction from the obvious—someone was trying to kill me.

I watched Aidan's face for clues. His mouth tightened. I put my fork down. My appetite had disappeared. The cup trembled in my hands as I took a sip of coffee. The heat stung my lips, which were sensitive from my teeth having bitten into them once too often.

After Aidan ended the call, he came and joined me at the table. He lowered himself onto the seat. His eyelids lifted, and I fell into his blue and troubled gaze.

"What's happening, Aidan? Is he dead?"

He shook his head. "Apparently, he escaped from the wreckage."

"So he's alive?"

He shrugged. "He must be."

"That's a relief," I murmured into my coffee.

"I would have preferred the asshole caught, myself."

"Me too. But at least my actions didn't cause a death," I said.

"Of course. I'm sorry. This has been so hard for you. And it's all because of me."

"Stop blaming yourself, Aidan. I don't see it that way. It's a small price to pay to be with you. If I had to choose, then I'd prefer to be in danger and be with you instead of being safe and not with you."

"Oh, my angel." He smiled sadly. "I'll do everything to keep you safe." Aidan held me. "There's something you must promise me. You must promise me not to drive. James must drive from now on, okay?"

I nodded with a tight, contrite smile.

"Would that have made a difference? We still would've been pursued, I imagine."

Aidan sighed. "Yeah, probably. Only James has got a gun."

A sudden lump made it difficult to swallow. "This is really getting dark, Aidan."

"That it is. I'm going to get to the bottom of it. Don't you worry, my love." He rose. "We have to go in now. Are you okay with that?"

"You bet. I want my dress back."

Aidan cast me one of those smiles that made all the drama playing out in my head evaporate.

I leaned in and kissed him feverishly, tongue and all.

He pulled back his head to look at me. His eyes had a lusty glow. "Hmm... That's better."

CHAPTER SEVEN

AIDAN

FROM THE MOMENT I received news of the car chase from my father, adrenaline thundered through me, just as it had in the fields of Afghanistan, plus more. Much more. I could've leaped over a building to get to Clarissa and hold her close. Protect her. That my beautiful girl was in danger due to my shitty past made my blood boil. I wanted to kill the motherfucker that was behind it.

Clarissa's squeal of delight after the cop handed her a parcel released some of the heaviness gripping me. Earlier, I'd heard her tell the cop that I wasn't allowed to see it. The policeman scratched his chin and agreed. When she added that it was her wedding dress, he peered up at me with an expression that said what I felt— "You're one lucky man."

But it was back to serious business. I gave some names to the cops. Bryce stood out for me. But then a creepy, ghostly finger slid down my spine as John Howard's ugly head entered my thoughts. The name of the sadistic husband of my former teacher was jotted down too.

As I entered the room that had become our love haven, a jagged breath left my lips. It was such a relief, being home with my beautiful girl. Clarissa sat at the balcony, sketching. What a sight— bare feet, a floral skirt, and a loose blouse, her hair up in a messy bun. I could have watched her all day. She calmed me. And I sure as hell needed some relief from my unsettled state of mind.

I joined her and peered over her shoulder at her sketch—a drawing of the garden. I bent down and planted a kiss on her long, slender neck.

She gazed up and smiled sweetly, turning her sketch over.

"Hey, I was looking at that," I protested.

"It's not ready yet. It's only a study. I'm going to do a watercolor of the same scene."

I'd seen her watercolors. They were magical, just like her. Clarissa had a ton of talent. Besides the bubble of pride that that generated, a sliver of insecurity lingered inside of me. Maybe she'd tire of me after meeting someone as talented as Chris and leave me. I'd even voiced that fear one night after a few tongue-loosening drinks. In response, Clarissa fell onto her knees and swallowed every last drop I had in me.

What was a man meant to do with that? Feel reassured, I suppose.

I stroked her arm, noticing she was braless. It was hard not to want to run my hands under her blouse. Our earlier lovemaking had done little to satisfy my appetite for her. I pushed my pelvis against her shoulder as my cock thickened.

Her big brown eyes went all melty with lust as she gazed up at me. Her skin puckered to my touch, and her nipples strained against her blouse, making my lips ache to taste them.

Clarissa giggled. "Aidan, I think my sketch has aroused you."

I laughed. "Even though I'm stimulated by its considerable artistic merit, it's more to do with the fact you're not wearing a bra, Clarissa." I raised a brow.

My hand went up her blouse, indulging in her warm, soft, full breasts which made my mouth water. "Why don't you step inside for a moment, sweetheart. The gardeners are out and about. And even though I love touching you in public, at home, it's different."

She rose and allowed me to lead her back inside. I couldn't help but sigh with pleasure over how our sexual appetites were perfectly matched. Waking up to Clarissa's warm, writhing body was a joy to behold. It had become an addiction for me because whenever I went away, my bed felt cold and empty. Not to mention the nightmares that magically disappeared whenever I wrapped my arms around her. Her warm breath, while she slept, was the sweetest, most comforting feeling on my skin.

In the mornings, I loved how she would move gently against me. As I spooned her, still half asleep, she would transport me to an erotic twilight zone. My cock was always hard and throbbing and her sweet little pussy always wet and ready.

I could have lost every dollar I owned, and I still would have been a happy man knowing that Clarissa was mine.

We were made for each other.

My hand traveled up her skirt and found her pussy naked. "Mm... I'm glad we're adhering to the no-panties rule." My fingers crept up her warm thighs and parted her damp lips, entering gently into that oh-so-perfect tight little pink opening. "Ah... princess, you feel nice and creamy."

Clarissa had her hand on my zipper and was about to free my throbbing cock when the phone buzzed. I had been waiting on a call from the cops, and I couldn't ignore it. "Damn, I've got to get that."

After I ended the call, my veins went from pumping hot to icy cold in a matter of seconds.

"What is it, Aidan?" asked Clarissa.

"Bryce is dead."

Clarissa's eyes widened. "What? Was he driving behind me? Did he die from the crash?"

"No. It wasn't him. He was in Vegas at the time of the accident."

"How did he die?"

"He was stabbed in an alleyway."

"In Vegas?" asked Clarissa in a shocked tone.

I shook my head. "No. Downtown. He was stabbed in the early hours of this morning. He must have flown back late last night." I grabbed my jacket. "I've got to go to the police station now."

"Do you want me to come?" she asked.

"No, beautiful girl, please stay here. I won't be long." I held her tight. My heart was beating fast. For once, it wasn't from being turned on.

· · · ● · ● · · ·

THE POLICE STATION HAD that Sunday-morning-after-hangover vibe. I could see it had been a big night. There were mainly young men in their late teens to early twenties, who'd obviously exerted their masculinity by fighting and showing that theirs was bigger. They straggled out. In the harsh light of day, they'd shrunk. Shuffling along, and regretful as they stared down at their feet.

An older man sat behind his desk, staring out the window, lost in thought. He turned and pointed to a chair. "Thanks for coming in so quickly. I'm Detective Max Hudson from the Homicide Special Section."

I shook his hand. "This is about Bryce Beaumont, I take it?"

"Yeah. As you know, he was found murdered early yesterday morning."

I nodded.

"We'll need to know your whereabouts."

Predictably, I was a suspect. Without flinching, I replied, "I was at my home in Malibu."

"Can anyone vouch for that?"

"Yes, my fiancée, cook, security guy, and maid."

"I'm aware that your fiancée, Clarissa Moone, was involved in a car-ramming incident on Friday evening."

I nodded. "Have you got any news on the driver?"

He shook his head. "All we've been able to ascertain from the wreckage is that it was a rented vehicle."

"You don't think Bryce could have been involved?"

"Nope. He was in Vegas at the time. We've got CCTV footage of him there to confirm that. He still had a plane ticket in his pocket when we found him dead. We traced credit card transactions back to a hotel in Vegas."

"He wasn't robbed when you found him?"

He shook his head. "He didn't have any cash on him, but his credit cards and license were found on him." He squared his shoulders. "Tell me about your relationship with the deceased."

I took a deep breath. "We were in the Special Forces together in Afghanistan. After I set up the Veterans' Health Center, I employed him to run it. I fired him after he caused trouble."

"Mm... that's the shortened version. You had him charged for an abduction attempt on your fiancée. He was out on bail when he was stabbed."

"Yeah, I know. I'm still wondering who bailed him out."

"All roads lead back to you, Thornhill."

I shook my head. "What do you mean?"

"Your ex-fiancée, Jessica Mansfield, paid one million big ones to bail him out. She was also sleeping with him at the time of his murder."

Even though that was old news for me, I kept that to myself.

"Okay, so she bailed him out."

"The night of Bryce's murder, your father left a message on the deceased's phone. I can tell you it wasn't for a pleasant chat. He left a threatening message."

His stare penetrated. He scrutinized my face, seeking clues, but I remained stone-cold sober. I was good at that, despite the internal haywire.

My father had known of Bryce's threats to bring down my empire. I recalled his suggestion to place a hit on Bryce after I expressed my frustration from buying his silence. Of course, that was no longer necessary. But Grant was not aware that I'd been exonerated. It had been a big month, and I hadn't had a chance to catch up with him, partly due to his lack of availability since he started bedding Tabitha.

"My father's many things, but a murderer he's not."

"There's one thing I've learned from this job. Many will murder to protect those they love. Bryce Beaumont was on the take. After your generous handouts stopped, he attempted to abduct your fiancée. Would you please explain why you were paying him large sums of money on a regular basis? Separate to his wage, of course."

I ran my fingers through my hair. Fuck. This was martial law now. I knew he was out of his jurisdiction. "Bryce was blackmailing me over an incident in Afghanistan."

He gesticulated for me to continue.

"It was an incident during an ambush, involving a fellow soldier. I have since been exonerated for it."

He nodded slowly. "You went through a military tribunal?"

Sweat dripped down my back. "Not as such. I reported it to my superior and was cleared of any wrongdoing. At the time, Bryce played on my guilt. I was distressed after our platoon was nearly wiped out. My best buddy lay dying. I had to put him out of his misery before the Taliban made minced meat of him by dragging him through the streets as a trophy. I might add, we were miles away from the evacuation zone and surrounded by insurgents."

His face pinched. Wearing the kind of haggard features of one who'd experienced the worst of humanity, Detective Hudson was an old man who looked as though he should have been at home, in slippers, reading the newspaper. "Sounds like a fucking nightmare. I was in 'Nam."

I drew a mock smile. "Vietnam wasn't exactly a walk in the park, either."

He nodded slowly. "You can say that again." He puffed out a loud breath. "Okay, then, back to your father."

"Detective Hudson, as I stated earlier, I can't see how Grant could have done this. His motive is not strong enough. You see, he's got a new, young, beautiful girlfriend. My father's a weak man when it comes to women. He's a hopeless romantic. I've never seen him as happy as he's been of late. I can't even begin to imagine him jeopardizing that by committing murder."

He closed his book. "Okay, that will do for now."

I stood up. "Can I bring in my own investigators with regard to the car incident? I need to know who's behind it."

His craggy brow lowered. "Have you got more enemies other than John Howard?"

Fuck. What didn't they know? "You know about that?"

He tilted his head. "Sure do. He's a brutish sonofabitch. And it's no secret that he's out for your scalp. I'd be stepping up security if I were you."

"Can't you lock up the fucker and throw away the key? He's a dirty prick."

"We know that. But he's done the time."

"Then why aren't you watching him?"

He sniffed. "In a city like this, if we watched every murderous asshole released from prison, we'd need to quadruple our men on the ground. In any case, it doesn't sound like the type of approach a violent murderer like Howard would take. Generally, with revenge, they like a slow, blood-churning approach so that they can watch their victim pleading all the way to the brutal end."

My stomach sank to my feet. The memory of Howard's savagery infested my spirit. On that cold note, I left the station with a heavy tread.

CHAPTER EIGHT

GRANT'S LOCAL HANGOUT, A dark, pokey little bar in Venice, was how I'd always remembered it. Still the same faces—lonely spirits seeking wisdom from other equally solitary figures, clutching their beers as if their lives depended on it. They did depend on it, as they depended on the gibbering counsel from others like them, which poured out in abundance like the beer they swallowed.

It had always been my father's little escape, particularly when he needed help. I preferred a shrink myself, but then who was I to judge? In the past, while my dad drank his demons away, I'd be in the home of some bored housewife, getting my cock sucked. I wasn't proud of my past predilection for older women. It wasn't so much that I preferred them, but that they were seriously hungry for cock. During this shameful phase of my life, I didn't have a favorite type. Young or old, tall or short, black or white, big or small, it didn't matter. They were all faceless to me.

As I reflected on that period of my life, I shuddered with revulsion. I had not only stained their sheets but their souls and mine.

"Hey, Aidan, good to see you," said Jimmy, the bartender. He'd been there for so long he'd melded into the bar and looked like a fixture. I was sure they'd bury him there.

Being someone who believed in loyalty and tradition, I appreciated Jimmy's smiling welcome. It gave off the same warm, fuzzy feeling as that of a kind, nonjudgmental uncle.

Grant came through the door. He was looking great. Tabitha had certainly put a charge in his step. He stood taller. I even noticed he'd lost some weight around his belly.

"Sorry, got caught up with my fucking neurotic neighbor."

"Do you want a beer?" I asked.

He jumped up on the stool and nodded a greeting to Jimmy. "Yeah, that would be great."

I made the order and took a sip of mine. "So, how's the new apartment?"

After Jimmy passed the large glass of amber fluid, Grant nearly drained it in one thirsty gulp. If anyone could drink, it was my father. He held it well. I'd never seen him drunk and unruly.

"It's shit. I hate it. I've got this fucking woman living below me. Every time I strum, and I mean strum the guitar—unplugged, quiet little fingerings— she gets her broom and bangs on the ceiling."

I shook my head and laughed. "That's pretty extreme."

"You're telling me." He finished off his beer and gesticulated to Jimmy for another. He looked at my half-full glass. "Do you want another?"

"Nope. I'm good. An apartment for a musician can be hard if you get the wrong neighbors."

"You're not kidding. It's mind-blowing, waking up to Tabitha. Don't get me wrong. I'm..." He tilted his head. His blue eyes had that familiar tinge of desire. Hmm... like father, like son. "I've fallen bad, Aidan."

"I can see that. I'm glad you gave the house to Sara. I like her a lot. She's family."

His mouth turned up at one end. "Yeah, me too. I felt so fucking guilty. I still do." He sighed. "Anyhow, the house was the least I could do. But you know, I've been with other women during my time with Sara."

I nodded. I couldn't decide if his addiction to casual sex was enough to exonerate him for breaking Sara's heart.

Reading my silence as censure, he said, "With Tabitha, it's different. For one, she told me she'd cut my balls off if I look at another woman. She's insanely jealous." He chuckled. "I like that. It means she's as crazy about me as I am about her."

"Tabitha's a wild one," I said.

"You're telling me. She's fucking hot."

"I mean she goes through her men quickly."

Grant shrugged. "It's a risk I'm willing to take. She's all over me, and living in an apartment for the first time in my life is kind of worth it. That's if I can find a way of dealing with the crazy dame below."

"But you need to practice, Dad. I've never known you not to."

He let out a frustrated breath. "Yeah. I do. It's a concern. I'm going to look into getting the walls soundproofed."

"I've got a better idea. I'll buy you a house," I said soberly.

His eyebrows knitted. "What? You would do that?"

"Why not? I can afford it. I've got an obscene amount of money."

He shook his head. "I'm so proud of you, Aidan. You're a legend. You would really do that? Buy me a house?"

"I bought Patti one, didn't I?"

"I have to say, it would be a relief to be on terra firma again. I'm not much into the apartment thing. Apart from the view of the sea, that is. I like pottering around in the garden amongst my little green bushes." He raised a brow.

My father loved growing weed. Only for personal use, as he always reassured me.

"I've got a few starting up on the balcony, but it's not the same."

"Find yourself a nice house. I'll buy it for you."

"How much can I spend?"

"Whatever you like. I just made a billion this week. I can afford it. Buy a big, rambling, two-story job. Set up a studio in it."

Grant got off his barstool and hugged me. "Thanks, son. That's so special. Considering I haven't always been there for you, especially when you were young. I don't deserve it."

"You gave me life, Dad."

"Yeah, you and God knows how many more." He downed his drink and beckoned for another.

I frowned. "What? Have I got a few siblings out there?"

"I'm not sure. Nobody's shown up as yet. You never know." His lips curled up slowly. "I've fucked many women. In my earlier days, the only plastic foils I opened were tobacco packets. Condoms were 1950s shit. You know? Before the pill." He chuckled.

I shook my head. "Then you've been fucking lucky, Dad."

"Haven't I?"

"Change of subject," I said, sitting forward. "Of a more gruesome nature. Bryce Beaumont is dead."

My father's grimace and wide-eyed surprise released the tightness I'd been carrying in my chest since leaving the police station. I'd learned from my army training how to read a face, especially when something dark hid behind the bullshit. I knew my father well, and right then, I knew, without doubt, that he couldn't have stabbed Bryce.

"How?" he asked.

"He was stabbed in Venice."

"A drug deal? He probably owed money."

I nodded. "I'd say so. That's what I told the detective. The thing is, they found a threatening message you sent Bryce. They're going to question you. You'll need an alibi."

"Fuck. I'm a suspect?"

I nodded.

"When was he murdered?"

"Early yesterday. I'm told it was around two in the morning."

Grant shrugged. "I was with Tabitha for dinner, then at the Red House doing a gig, as usual. I was there jamming until at least three in the morning."

"I told them that you were doing a gig. Anyway, expect a call from the cops."

"Then it wasn't Bryce driving?" Grant asked.

"Nope. He was in Vegas the night before. The following night, he was back here and murdered. Of course, the motives are all over us. Can't say I blame them for thinking that considering the timing."

He nodded reflectively. "Yeah, for sure, I can see how it looks." He rolled a cigarette. "Who was driving that car, then?"

"I wish I fucking knew. They've checked all the hospitals for injuries that came in around that night. Nothing. It's a shitty little mystery. Unless he fell into the water and the waves took him. I've considered that."

"Tabitha replayed the whole episode to me. I must say, Clarissa did well."

Respect and love emanated from me. "Yeah, she did. She's quiet and seriously sensitive. But she's strong when called for. You heard how she kneed Bryce in the balls when he tried to abduct her?"

"I did. Tabitha and Clarissa are pretty thick."

"Don't I know it."

"I somehow sense that you don't trust Tabitha."

"She changes her men as regularly as her panties, and it's been hard for me to get over Evan."

Grant hung his head. "That was insanely tragic. Aidan, I know he was a good friend. But he was also a savage toward her. When I first got with Tabitha, she was black and blue."

"Yeah, that sadomasochism shit."

Grant scratched his chin. "I know she's got flaws. But I'm willing to take the risk. She's one hell of a woman."

I smiled. "As long as you're happy, Dad, and as long as you know the score. Then it's all good."

"Have you got any theories on who was driving that car?"

"It was probably a hire job. A hitman, maybe."

"A hitman? You'd think he'd be able to handle the wheel a bit better."

"The PCH is a notorious stretch. Especially at night, with rising moisture from the sea."

"That's true. Who do you think could've been behind it?"

"It's obviously John Howard. The cops are about to question him."

"Ah, him. Shit. Aidan, you need to step up your security, man."

"I was seriously pissed at Clarissa for driving. She's meant to have James driving her. And I've got Linus at home, watching over us."

"But what about now, your own day-to-day life?"

"I'm all right."

"Are you carrying a gun?"

"I've got one in the car," I said.

Grant touched my arm. "Aidan, promise me you'll be careful. If anything happened to you? Then I would fucking kill, for sure."

I smiled. "That won't be necessary, Dad."

"Tabitha tells me you're marrying around your birthday. November. That's not far away. Four weeks."

"The sooner, the better."

Grant nodded. "I can understand that. Clarissa's a one-off. And you are really well suited."

"She's the best thing that's ever happened to me. I say that without any reservation."

"Yeah, well, that's saying something, considering you're one of LA's richest men."

I smiled.

"Is it going to be held at the estate? Something like Greta's?"

"Yeah. Although to be honest, I don't feel like a big bash. If I had it my way, it would be just the two of us on the beach. That's where it all started for us."

"I thought you met on the job, so to speak."

"I employed her to be my PA. But we first got together on my yacht."

"Nice."

"It was more than nice." I looked down at my hands. My body heated up as I recalled that night. It was etched in my soul. I looked up at my father. "I was her first, you know?"

He was rolling a cigarette and stopped to look up at me. "You're kidding me."

I shook my head slowly.

"Wow. I've never been with a virgin before." He stared at me as if I'd visited something mystical and consecrated.

"That surprises me with your track record," I said.

He laughed. "Like you, I lost my virginity to an older woman. And from that point on, most women I fucked were enthusiastic partners, if you know what I mean."

"Yeah, loose and wild. I know the type well. Been there, done that."

He patted my arm. "Like father, like son." He lit his cigarette and stared at me with an awkward quizzical expression. "What was it like?"

It was a question I'd never been asked, so I needed time to think. My body remembered, though, for blood raced through my veins. "It was incredible."

He nodded slowly. "Right. Was it as good as they say?"

"Who's they?" I asked.

"You know how it's the fantasy of many to have a virgin." He grinned.

"Although I broke every rule in my book by going there, there's nothing that I can compare it to. Especially where someone like Clarissa is involved. Hers is the type of beauty that I'd endure the twelve labors of Hercules to win."

He laughed. "Then all those muscles upon muscles that your Special Force training gave you were for a good cause because if anyone could wrestle a tiger, it would be you."

I chuckled. "It was a lion, Dad."

"Same thing, really, in the dangerous beasts' stakes." He cast me a wry grin. "So it was that good, eh?"

"Apart from a sensation that is beyond exquisite, it's the giving, you know? The sacrifice. It's like this person trusts me so much to suffer this pain."

He grimaced. "Was she in pain?"

"Yeah, she was. But that didn't last." My heart raced. I'd just revealed something extremely intimate, and although it was my father, it felt forbidden but releasing all at the same time.

He smiled. "I can now understand why you're so in love with her."

"Purity is a powerful drug. Knowing that you've experienced something that no other ever has or ever will defies words."

"That's why poetry was invented," said Grant.

I nodded thoughtfully. "Clarissa is poetry."

My father smiled wistfully.

We finished our drinks in silent reflection.

I rose from the stool. "I've got to go, Dad. As soon as you find a home you like, let me know, and I'll write the check."

We hugged.

"Thanks, son," he said.

"Don't worry. I've got heaps of money."

"I meant thanks for sharing your first time with me." He had a tear in his cheek. Fuck. I'd never seen that before.

I couldn't speak for fear of crying myself. It was strangely moving. We hugged again.

I saluted Jimmy and headed back to my angel in paradise.

CHAPTER NINE

---◆◇◆---

CLARISSA

TABITHA DRAGGED ME ALONG. As always, she was full of bounce. After I'd dangled my Victoria's Secret card in front of her, she shrilled, "Let's go there right now."

She sniffed the air as we entered the lingerie haven. "Smell that, Clary. Pure sex."

I rolled my eyes. "Do you ever think of anything else?"

"Yeah, of course, like your wedding."

"Hmm... about that."

She stopped walking. "What?"

"Aidan wants a smallish affair."

"Smallish? In what sense?"

"Just the inner sanctum. You know, about twenty guests or so."

"And that's all?"

I nodded.

"Then you don't need me for anything." Her tone was flat.

"I need you to be there. I'd love for you to hang out with me while I'm getting ready."

Her lips formed a tight smile. "I can do that, easy enough." She looked up at me with a guilty smile. "Can we at least have a wild girls' night?"

"As long as it doesn't involve a male stripper or some leather-panted dude named Fabio."

She laughed. "I'm a bit more imaginative than that. What about a burlesque show, or one of those..."

"What?"

"I've heard about these S and M dungeons."

"Are you kidding me? After everything that's happened?"

She tilted her head. "I hated being beaten. But when it was just a little whipping here and there, that was really sexy as hell, to be honest."

Oh no. Was Tabitha getting restless again? "Let me ask you something."

"What's that?" She flicked through a rack of bras.

"Are you getting bored with Grant?"

She looked up. Her face scrunched. "Are you kidding? He's hot and delicious. No way. There's something about an older, experienced man that just makes me feel sexy as hell." She held up a green bra. "What do you think of this color?"

"Love it. Goes perfectly with your eyes. Pop it in." I pointed to the cart.

"I'll have to try it first. Are you sure you don't mind?"

"Sweetie, I've got an open account here. I haven't been here for months. So let's go to town. Aidan made me promise I would."

She coughed out a laugh. "I bet he did. Tell me, is he still destroying your panties?"

"When I wear them." A little curl formed on my lips.

She put her arm around my shoulders. "Ah... that's my friend. You're learning fast. Wear sexy, barely-there panties when out, and at home wear none. It's a trusty method."

I got goose-fleshed as I recalled Aidan's ravaging tongue the previous night while we sat on the sofa watching a movie. My sex pulsed. It was only a few hours ago he took me in the shower, all hard and hungry. Something I'd discovered about my ardent lover was that in the mornings, he was at his most savage best, while in the evenings he was tender and deliciously slow—passionate tongue kisses that trailed over my prickly skin, leaving me deliriously high after multiple mind-altering orgasms. That was unless we hadn't seen one another for a day or so. Then it would be a clothes-ripping session of feverish sex.

Tabitha dangled a white lace bustier with little red floral buttons. "Hey, this is sweet and has a vintage feel. Just up your alley."

"That's really cute." As usual, I let Tabitha make the choices. She knew me well. I was just happy to amble along with my head in the clouds, indulging in a swelling ache as I contemplated Aidan's lusty gaze when I modeled the scanty underwear.

She held up a red lace teddy with a lace-up front against me. "What about that?"

That would be a good one for when we got all hot and steamy on Skype. I wiped my brow. Mm... who would have thought a walk through a sexy lingerie shop could be so arousing?

Tabitha stopped at a pink bra-and-panty set and cooed.

"Pop it in, Tabs. It's yours."

We left with an armful of shopping bags. Skipping along, Tabitha said, "That was so much fun. Thanks, Clary. I hope Aidan won't mind. It was a huge spend."

"He won't. He doesn't care about money."

She pulled her head back. "Really?" She smiled. "Is this real? Are we really this happy? And in love?"

I giggled. "I keep asking myself that all the time."

"The house is beautiful, Clary. You liked it, didn't you?"

"I sure did."

"I've never lived in anything like it. I've been always holed up in apartments. As you know." Her voice cracked.

I stopped walking and looked at her. "We've both got guardian angels out there, I'd say."

She hugged me. "I'm so glad you're here. I don't know what I'd do without my little sister."

My eyebrows squeezed tight. "Little? We're the same age."

She pulled my hair playfully and giggled. "Let's go back to my lovely new house. I'll make us a martini."

"A martini?"

"Why not? James is driving."

"Let's," I said, taking her arm. "Which reminds me, do you want to come to New York with me?"

Tabitha screamed so loudly, everyone on the pavement stopped. "When?"

"Next week. Aidan asked if I wanted to go. He'll be dealing with business. He suggested I take you along so we can shop and share the experience."

"He suggested that?"

I nodded.

"Oh my God. That's so kind of him and seriously cool. I hope Grant can live without me. For how long?"

"A couple of days," I said.

"Yay!" Tabitha put her arm around me.

James was there, waiting patiently for us. He opened the car door on our approach, and I noticed Tabitha casting him a flirtatious smile.

"Thanks, James," I said, sliding onto the front seat. I refused to sit in the back. It was hard enough getting used to being driven around. But Aidan had been adamant. He went on about it repeatedly, so I relented and accepted my lot. It was a small price to pay for safety. And it meant I could go to Tabitha's new home and have a martini.

· · · • · • • · · ·

THIS WAS MY SECOND visit to Tabitha's new home in Venice. It was a wooden two-story blue house. I loved it. The garden was filled with trees and flourishing bushes. The interior had been renovated with the latest must-have amenities in the kitchen, and the open-space living area was fitted with French doors that opened out onto a patio and swimming pool.

Tabitha popped her shopping bags on the table and headed straight to the kitchen to mix us a drink.

"This is such a lovely place, Tabs."

"Isn't it? And the kitchen's so easy to get around in."

"How are your cooking classes going?" I asked.

"I've stopped."

"What happened to the goddess in the kitchen and the..."

"The slut in the bedroom," she said, finishing my sentence. "I'm definitely the latter. But cooking's not that natural for me. I have learned how to flip an omelet, though." She nodded, looking pleased with herself.

"That's a major achievement, considering your omelets always ended up as scrambled eggs." I laughed.

"I hope I'm enough for Grant." Tabitha's lips twisted into a wistful smile. She poured the gin and vermouth into a silver shaker and was about to stir it when I grabbed her hand.

"Shaken, not stirred." I raised a brow, and she laughed raucously at my James Bond impersonation.

"I always get that mixed up." She rattled the shaker. "But seriously, Clary, do you think I can make this work?" Her hands did a sweep in the air.

"Of course, you can."

"You don't think I'll fuck it up somehow, do you?" Her eyes pooled with uncertainty.

"As long as you don't hire a gardener who goes around shirtless, you should be safe."

She laughed. "Now that's an idea. One can't live in the suburbs without ogling a sexy, tanned torso bending over the petunias or cleaning the pool."

"I suppose there's no harm in ogling."

She poured out our martinis and handed me a glass. I took a sip and grimaced.

"Too strong?" she asked.

"Probably. But one will do." I stepped into the living space. The sofa faced out to the pool area and garden. "This is a gorgeous house. I get such a good vibe. It's really relaxing sitting here."

"I love it, too. I've never felt this stable before." Her lips turned down.

"Are you having doubts? I told you it was too soon."

"No, I'm not, really. Grant's sexy and gorgeous, and he holds me, and I can't imagine not having him around forever."

I nodded. "But?"

"I get off on fantasies that are a bit twisted." She took a sip. "Is that wrong? You know, while he's fucking me?" Her eyes shone with guilt.

I shrugged. Before Aidan, I was the queen of twisted fantasies. I wasn't sure what side of morality that put me. "Not sure. It depends on the fantasy, I suppose."

She sipped her martini pensively. "I think I'm into the whole submissive thing. Being tied up, blindfolded, all of that."

"Have you shared that with Grant?"

"Kind of. But the Evan episode is still a bit raw. And I'm worried he'll connect it to him, seeing that Evan introduced me to that world."

I sighed. "I don't know what to say. I mean, I'm just pretty standard when it comes to my sexual needs."

"You mean, you're vanilla."

I sniffed. "You say that as if it's boring sex. Let me tell you, friend of mine, that a day rarely goes by in which I haven't had multiple ceiling-banging orgasms."

"Ha... me too. Grant has an expressive tongue and a really big..." She gesticulated with her hands.

"Okay, okay. That's my father-in-law-to-be you're talking about."

"So you keep saying. But I need my little best friend to talk to about such things as big dicks, weird sex acts, and the like."

"Weird sex acts?" Now she had me curious.

"Not so weird, but I'm working on it."

"If you feel the need to share details of your debauchery with me, I will be there. I promise. Only warn me so I can think of Grant as a man and not family. That bit is still strange to me."

Tabitha chuckled. "You'll get used to it, I'm sure. Anyway, you've locked in this Sunday for our housewarming party, I hope? It's going to be a hoot. Grant knows tons of people, and I've invited Johnny and his new girl. And..." She smiled. "I'm going to prepare some food."

I'll come over early and help if you like," I suggested.

Her face lit up. "Would you? That would be so much fun."

"Of course. I'm sure Aidan won't mind. He's pretty taken with the house. And there's a pool table. He loves his pool."

"Do you play with him? You were never that good. Remember at college?"

I nodded. "I haven't improved. But Aidan likes to play with me because he's one big perv."

"Uh-huh... let me guess. Bending over the large table? With or without panties?"

My face heated up. Even around my dirty-minded friend, it still made me blush to summon up memories of our pool nights, which had become a favorite pastime for Aidan. I shifted my position. I'd gone sticky, thinking about how Aidan pushed himself against my naked behind.

"Now that doesn't sound that vanilla," sang Tabitha.

CHAPTER TEN

———◆◇◆———

TABITHA AND HER SEX-LADEN chatter had me arriving home aroused. The martini had helped. The first thing I did was drop in on Aidan in his music room. I found him ripping into one of his wild licks. I loved hearing the raw and raucous notes bouncing off the walls and how his pelvis pushed hard against the back of the red guitar as if he were making love to it.

I wiped my brow. His bulging biceps flexed, all veiny and hard, while his fingers ran up and down the fretboard. His hair had fallen onto his face, his eyes were closed, and those luscious sculptured lips, apart and moist. Mm... I'd seen that look before.

He opened his big blue eyes, and as always, robbed me of air. Would he ever stop doing that to me? I wondered. He was about to put his guitar down, but I shook my head and motioned for him to continue playing.

Aidan was an avid musician. When he wasn't running his business, he was in his studio, firing up his guitar. There were also quieter, reflective moments when he'd balance his acoustic guitar on his muscular thighs, exploring new riffs. He had so much talent I wondered why Aidan wasn't a professional musician.

But then, bristling at the thought of women throwing themselves and their panties at him, I was glad he wasn't. As selfish as that seemed.

By his own admission, Aidan suffered from stage fright, which came as a surprise. It didn't show at my father's wedding or at the Red House, where I first watched him perform. I told him as such, but he just shrugged it off and spoke of his newfound passion for writing songs.

I loved watching him place dots on sheet music. I quickly learned that Aidan was equally as driven and focused on music as he was in his business. If not more. His virtuosity and flair made him one truly gifted musician. I'd lost track of how many times I told him that. He'd just smile and deny it. It wasn't false modesty. Aidan was blessed with humility.

Was there anything about Aidan that was rotten?

His temper wasn't great. But then, without fire in his belly, he would not be such a smoking-hot lover.

Dressed in my silk chinoiserie, I decided to treat Aidan and model one of my lacy purchases. The red lace teddy sent a feverish shiver through me at the thought of what Aidan would do to me. Rather fittingly, I was stretched out on the chaise longue, reading erotic short stories by Anaïs Nin.

Aidan entered the room and cast me one of his irresistible smiles. "I think it's time we get Chris to do a painting of you like that."

I pointed to the many studies of Aidan and me already on the walls. "I don't know if I could stand another painting of me," I replied.

"I could. And you look like something out of a dream at the moment."

"Instead of me, I'd like a painting of you playing your guitar. You look so sexy when you play."

He smiled sweetly. "Maybe."

I placed my book down and watched him approach me. Aidan wore a Led Zeppelin T-shirt that stretched around his big shoulders, while his jeans hugged his strong thighs.

I took a deep breath and inhaled his scent of herbal shampoo and male, which, as always made me dissolve. Blood pumped down below my navel as I made room for him on the chaise longue.

He undid my hair, making it cascade over my shoulders. His hand stroked my neck then crept down my shoulders. Hungry for his fingers, my flesh puckered while, straining against the lace, my nipples hardened.

Aidan's heavy gaze reflected my longing. His fingers slid over the slippery silk that covered me. He ran his tongue along my lower lip before settling on my mouth. His lips, warm and moist, softened on contact before crushing mine as passion took over. Our tongues swam together. I loved tasting him and how he played with me so suggestively. I'd forgotten to breathe.

As his hand slipped under my silk gown, I exhaled tightly. When he felt the roughness of the lace he undid the tie of my gown, and like water, it fell to my feet.

He hissed. His eyes darkened with lust. "Baby, let me look at you."

My breasts poured out of the skimpy outfit.

"Stand up and dance for me, princess."

Aidan went and sat on the bed ready for my little performance. I sashayed toward him, and he opened his legs to make room for his hardening cock. I stood before him and swayed my hips.

"Mm... that's so sexy," he rasped.

As my hips gyrated in front of him, he unzipped his jeans. He kicked his jeans off, and I saw his eager cock pleading to be freed.

"T-shirt." I pointed at his torso.

He lifted it over his head, and my eyes moved from his eyes to that rippling pectorals and to his cock.

My thighs were damp as I watched his glistening cock, bluey red, veins distended. I salivated. His heady, earthy scent of male arousal was like a drug. I pulsated with the pain of excitement.

I sat on his lap and placed my breasts in his face, my nipples aching for his hungry mouth.

"You set me on fire. The more of a woman you become, the sexier. And these tits make me so hard." His face buried into my breasts, his hot lips and tongue leaving trails of warm moisture over my nipples. Instead of undoing the lace to my teddy, he pulled it off roughly, making the delicate fabric rip, freeing my heated flesh.

Just like all my lingerie, my little outfit lasted barely a few minutes around Aidan. There were plenty where that came from, I thought, quietly amused. That was part of the game, dancing around until he was so engorged with need, he became animalistic.

His ravishing tongue drove inside me. A moan trembled through me. His hands grasped my bottom as he groaned into my sex. My fingers twirled deliriously through his hair as I pushed his head deeply into me. He fluttered his tongue over my bud, sucking and licking, one flickering impulse after another until I turned to jelly and quivered a creamy release into his mouth.

He wiped his mouth on my thigh. "It's music. Hearing you come. Your sweet little whimpers that build into groans send my cock crazy, angel."

If his tongue and fingers were earth-shattering, then the thought of having him entering me, shook the very foundation of my whole universe.

I stroked his throbbing cock. It was lubricated with pre-cum and I licked the head. Aidan moaned and fell back on the bed. I took him in deep, having learned to relax my throat. He was so big my mouth stretched to its limits.

"Ah..." he groaned. I could smell his build-up. I knew when he was about to erupt, for the veins pulsated on my tongue. He pulled out. "It's making me want to blow. Open your legs wide. Let me look at your drenched little cunt." I did as he asked, and he held his cock in his hand. "Play with yourself, baby."

My finger circled around my swollen button.

He held up two fingers. "Enter yourself."

His eyes were ablaze with arousal. I was so wet that my fingers slid in and out. He took my finger and sucked it. "Your tight little pussy is made of honey, sexy girl."

He placed me on all fours, and on his knees, he positioned himself against me. I loved being taken this way. It was so deep, setting off an agonizing ache through me.

"I need to go hard, Clarissa."

"Please," I whimpered.

His hands cupped my breasts as he thrust into me sharply. I gasped at the pleasurable stretch. My head dropped back and my eyes watered from the delicious ache. I was tingly and my blood hot. Every nerve was on edge, letting off little sparks. The friction was intense as he pounded into me. Aidan's breath was rough and uneven. His groans turned into growls as he took me with the need of one who'd been starved, which wasn't the case, considering I'd swallowed an eruption out of him for breakfast.

As he drove hard into me, stars poured down behind my eyes. The build-up soared as his rampaging cock found new zones to rub against. Each thrust made my muscles spasm uncontrollably, as I clenched his hardness tight. I lifted off and came back. Each time I stayed away longer until I became such a dribbling mess that I surrendered entirely and was swept by a hot wave of time-stretching bliss. My moans lengthened into a scream as my body convulsed in pleasure that swallowed me whole. He trembled through his own thunderous orgasm.

We crashed into each other's arms.

When we returned back to earth, Aidan kissed me tenderly.

He laid on his side and pushed hair away from my face. "You're so damn addictive. I can't get enough of you, my love."

"I feel the same. You leave me breathless."

· · ● ● ● ● ● ● · ·

The silver Art Deco lamp of a girl in an arabesque pose, holding a ball, sat beautifully in Tabitha's new home. I'd brought it as a house-warming gift after recalling her enthusiasm for it at the auction.

"I love it." She hugged me.

Tabitha went outside looking for Grant, who was showing Aidan his garden. "Come and have a look at what Clarissa and Aidan have given us."

Grant wiped his hands on his jeans. "Not more gifts. I would've thought giving us the house was enough," he said, looking at Aidan.

Aidan shrugged. "It was Clarissa's idea. Not that I mind. We've got a truckload of them at home. But they're very attractive. One can't really have enough beautiful things." He looked at me. "Didn't you bring something else also?"

I nodded. "James left it at the door."

"Something else?" Tabitha frowned. "You spoil me, Clary." She followed me out. Two wrapped paintings balanced against the wall.

She held her chin. "Now, let me guess..."

"They may surprise you," I said.

Aidan carried them in and placed them on the table.

"Come on. Open them," I said.

She ripped off the paper, and her eyes widened in surprise when she saw herself as the subject in both of the paintings. One depicted Tabitha on her stomach and the other sitting in a chair, leaning on her elbow, with a hint of a smile flickering in her large green eyes. They were nude studies that I'd produced while attending life-drawing classes where I'd arranged for Tabitha to model.

I remembered that occasion well. One could have almost cut the air with a knife. It had been that thick with desire. And the male students' heavy breathing was almost palpable as they kept dropping their implements, their faces flushed. Naturally, it was considered taboo to objectify the model in life-drawing classes, but with curvaceous Tabitha acting the coquette, their arousal was understandable.

"Oh my God, you colored them in. They're so pretty. Although..." Her lips drew into a tight line. "My butt looks a bit big."

I laughed. "I knew you'd say that."

Grant grabbed her by the waist and kissed her. "It's perfect. They're beautiful pictures. I love the colors and the way you've worked in the background." He cast a cheeky grin at Tabitha. "And the model's not bad either. Kind of sexy. Mm... really sexy." While he held Tabitha close, Grant directed his attention back to me. "Clarissa, I didn't know you were such a talented artist."

"I'm not sure about being talented. But it was Aidan who encouraged me to finish them, so I decided to add watercolor to them. It's become my favorite medium." I glanced up at Aidan with a shy smile. His blue eyes twinkled back with admiration.

Aidan turned to his father. "I made Clarissa show me her drawing folio, and when I saw these, I suggested she make a gift of them to you. This is the first time I've seen them in their finished state. They're really well done."

Not well-practiced at receiving compliments, I bowed my head with a faint smile and cast my attention back to Tabitha. "What do you really think?"

"I love them. I just wish my butt didn't look so big."

Grant laughed. "Your butt doesn't look big. I feel like pinching it." He patted her ass, and she giggled. "You look gorgeous, sweetheart. Perhaps a little skinnier than now."

She frowned. "What do you mean?"

I shook my head ever so slightly at Grant. But I could tell by his cheeky grin that he was playing with her. "You've put on weight in all the right places, baby."

He held her tight, and Tabitha dissolved into his hold.

Aidan whispered, "You're so talented you make my heart melt and my cock hard."

I whispered back, "You're insatiable."

His blue eyes shimmered with humor as blood coursed down to my sex, sending an ache, a delicious reminder of his needy thrusts earlier that day.

Grant rubbed his hands together. "How about a quick game of pool before the guests arrive?"

Aidan nodded with enthusiasm and followed his father.

I followed Tabitha into the kitchen. Pottering around preparing food gave me joy. In many ways, I missed that side of my life. Although I really couldn't complain. It was a small price to pay for being with Aidan. And with all the quality fresh meals I ate, my health glowed, while giving me stamina for my ravenous lover.

"What should I do?" I asked Tabitha, watching her pour two cups of coffee.

"Not sure." She shrugged, "Grant prepared a ton of burgers that will be grilled outside, as well as sausages for hot dogs. I suppose we can make a salad." She gaped at me blankly, twisting her mouth downward. "To be honest, I'm not sure where to start."

"Easy-peasy, Tabs."

She put her arm around me. "You're the best. I don't know what I'd do without you. If it wasn't for you, none of this would exist." Her voice quivered.

"You're not going to cry, are you?" I asked.

She shook her head and a faint smile chased away her frown. Her mood flipped, just like the Tabitha I'd always known and loved. She rubbed her hands together. "What will I chop?"

I grabbed the chopping board and brought out some tomatoes. "Start with these. I'll do the onions."

We danced about the kitchen, chopping away, throwing things at each other, and clowning about. One hour later, we'd made a green salad, coleslaw, potato salad, and bean salad.

Although I'd forgotten how tiring food preparation could be, I had a ball, as did Tabitha, who took to my instructions eagerly. Aidan had offered to have the party catered, but when Grant said he wanted to make his special burgers, Aidan's face lit up. According to Aidan, Grant's burgers were legendary.

CHAPTER ELEVEN

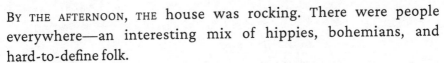

By the afternoon, the house was rocking. There were people everywhere—an interesting mix of hippies, bohemians, and hard-to-define folk.

"Grant knows a lot of people," I said to Aidan, who was diving into his second burger.

"He's been in the area all his life. These are the friends he's collected. The weed and music scenes, you know?" He smiled, then took another bite.

"The burgers are delicious," I said, tapping my belly. I'd already had one and felt seriously full.

"Aren't they? This is the best batch. I think Grant's making up for all those years living with Sara, who's a vegan, as you know." He laughed.

"I hope the vegans here are fine with the salads."

Aidan sniffed. "Well, if they're not, they can always forage in the garden." His droll delivery nearly made me spit out my drink. I squeezed my lips and swallowed, before holding my belly and giggling.

Aidan looked at me and laughed.

A woman literally bounced over to us. She wasn't wearing a bra and was very busty. She leaned in and kissed Aidan on the cheek, lingering a little more than was appropriate, I thought.

"It's so nice to see you again." She pulled away and looked at him properly. "You've gotten bigger." She touched his arm. The 'bigger' left her cushiony lips suggestively.

My fingernails dug into my palm.

Aidan smiled and directed his attention to me. "This is my fiancée, -Clarissa."

She stretched out her ring-cluttered hand. "Pleased to meet you." Her heavily kohled dark eyes wandered over my body. I wore a yellow polka-dot dress that Tabitha had, unsurprisingly, accused me of raiding my grandmother's wardrobe for.

"Sweet little dress." She stretched her words lazily as if she was stoned, which she probably was, considering the plume of weed smoke filling the air, and making me lightheaded.

Her sandalwood fragrance was so overpowering that it shot up my nasal passage, punching out all other scents. Although she was much older than Aidan, she was striking, with long black hair, olive skin, and big brown eyes. Her ample breasts spilled out of a black velvet dress. Recalling Aidan's earlier predilection for older, busty women, the green-eyed monster pounced on me.

"What have you been up to?" Her eyes flickered flirtatiously.

"I've been getting a renewable-energy program together," he replied. As she stepped closer, Aidan stepped away. He glanced over at me with a reassuring smile.

Reluctant to be seen as jealous and possessive, I left them to converse alone and joined Tabitha, who was busy flirting. She'd cornered a young, very good-looking boy.

He turned, and when he saw me his eyes warmed.

"Hey, Clarissa. This is Justin. He's one of Grant's guitar students."

I nodded a greeting. "I didn't know Grant taught."

"He teaches here. He's got heaps of students," said Tabitha.

Justin rested his interested gaze on me. Tabitha gave me a side glance and giggled. "Can you excuse us a minute, Justin?"

He'd lost his ability to talk and shuffled off.

"He's got the hots for you, Clary. As soon as you turned up, the poor boy lost his tongue. You do that to men, you know."

"And so do you, especially in those tight jeans and that low-cut blouse. God, Tabs, your boobs are getting bigger."

It was as if I'd told her she'd won the grand lottery. Her eyes shone. "Do you really think so?"

"You bet. You must be a C cup."

"Not like your gorgeous D cups," she returned, pulling down my bodice to expose some cleavage.

"What are you doing?" I asked.

"Just trying to show off some of your assets. You should be flaunting them. Like Morticia over there, talking to Aidan. Instead, you look like fucking Marcia Brady."

I looked over at Aidan. "She's really trying to seduce him, isn't she?" My unsubtle friend's head turned sharply in his direction.

"Don't make it so obvious, Tabs."

"That's Penelope. She plays the keyboards," she said.

"You've met her?"

"Yep. A few times. She's a groupie. She fucks everyone."

My burger sat uncomfortably in my gut suddenly. "Do you think she's been with Aidan? She's certainly standing close to him and acting very familiar."

"Maybe." Tabitha grabbed me by the arm. "Hey, he's crazy about you. And you can't think about all the women he's fucked before you. It will send you mad."

"I suppose." She was right. I recalled Aidan referring to that period of his life as BC. I had been so puzzled, I quizzed him, and he pointed out that it meant "before Clarissa." Aidan didn't hide that he'd made cringe-worthy choices and that sex for him used to be a sport.

Nevertheless, it came as a relief when Grant approached Aidan and whispered something to him. Aidan nodded and left Penelope be. I watched them head over to their instruments in the corner of the room, where they'd been set up for a jam.

A man with striped pants and a purple shirt skipped over to us.

"Here comes Mr. Hippy," whispered Tabitha.

I chuckled.

"Hey, girls." His glassy eyes darted from me to Tabitha and back again. I had to try hard not to giggle in his face because Tabitha positioned herself behind him and started pulling faces. I hated her for doing that. Not only for mocking the poor guy but because she was making it hard for me to keep a straight face.

He didn't seem to mind. "I'm Simon," he said, reading my tight smile as welcoming and encouraging.

"I'm Clarissa, and this is Tabitha." I moved closer to kick her gently on the leg.

"So, girls, can I interest you in a nice juicy spliff?" he asked.

The way he made "juicy" sound sexual made my skin crawl. Tabitha linked her arm with mine.

His eyebrows bounced with a hint of sleaze.

"No, we're not smokers," said Tabitha.

"I've got some cookies," he persisted.

"No, thanks. We'll stick to champagne."

He stared down at my chest when he spoke. I wasn't sure what he babbled, but I was pleased when Aidan came over and wrapped his arm around me. He acknowledged the languid stoner. "Hey, Simon."

"Aidan, how are you, man? This is a great shindig."

"It is. Can you excuse us for a moment?"

He led me away, leaving Tabitha with Simon, who I noticed was sporting a bulge, which was hard to miss in his figure-hugging pants. Gross.

"Although he's a sleaze, Simon's not a bad guy," said Aidan.

"Yeah, he's a bit icky," I said, letting Aidan lead me into the garden. "Where are we going?"

"We're about to start playing. I saw you standing there in that yellow dress, and when the wind lifted it slightly, it made me hard."

I giggled. "Aidan. You're consistently turned on."

"That's your doing, princess." His hand went up my dress. "You look smoking hot it this little dress." He ran his hands roughly over my satiny panties and squeezed my butt.

"Tabitha says I look like a 1950s spinster."

"Bullshit. You, darling girl, have got great taste. You're so sexy in that little dress, I want to fuck you here and now." He pushed me in against him. I could feel his hard rod against my thigh.

He went to hook his finger in my panties, and I placed my hand on his arm. "No, don't tear them off. I don't want to be without panties. This dress might fly up."

Aidan's eyes hooded. "Now that's every man's wet dream. But you're right. I don't want every guy at this party to see your glorious ass. You're already driving them crazy." He leaned in and ran his hands hungrily over my breasts, planting a clit-swelling kiss.

We heard rustling in the bushes and separated. Aidan played with my braids, and his eyes rested on my chest. "Your nipples are sticking out, baby."

I tried to tame them by rubbing them. "That's your doing, Aidan."

"I want you all the time, Clarissa." He squeezed my breasts. "These tits, this body, those eyes..." He held me so close I could feel him throbbing against my thigh. "You've bewitched me, angel."

Grant became visible. "There you are," he said. "We're about to start." He looked about the garden. "It's lovely in here, isn't it?"

"Yeah, I was about to fertilize it for you," said Aidan, grinning at me.

My face heated. I slapped him on the arm.

Aidan had his arm around my waist, as we followed Grant back inside.

The music, as always, was contagiously danceable. It was raw blues rock at its supreme best. Aidan was a sex-god up there, as his pelvis pushed against his guitar. Biting his bottom lip, he ripped into a wild guitar solo.

We swayed, skipped, and giggled uncontrollably, dancing with wild abandon. The music was so electric that everyone let their hair down and went wild.

"Morticia's in fine form," Tabitha shouted in my ear.

I looked in her direction, and like a belly dancer, she gyrated her hips seductively. She moved her head about, her hair flying out, as did her dress. Her eyes were on Aidan. But then, all of the women's eyes were on him.

With his back arched, he played his guitar as if he were making love to it. It was so erotic. I forgave any of them for swooning. As Morticia turned around and around, she could have easily been presiding over a witch's coven. Her black dress cascaded out, revealing shapely thighs.

Justin came and joined us, as did Sleazy Simon. It was fun. Tabitha was at her insouciant best, moving about without a care. She spun me around so that my little dress, fitted with a circular skirt, ballooned out. She did it one time too many because I noticed Aidan's eyes narrow.

Still, I liked him possessing me because I was hopelessly possessed.

• • • • • • • • • •

As James drove us home along the winding highway, Aidan, with his arms around me, noticed my body tighten.

He turned to look at me. "Are you okay?"

I gripped his hand. "It's the hour. It brings it all back."

"I'm so sorry. There's been so much drama lately. I haven't even asked

you how you were feeling about it all. You just seemed to be yourself."

"I've been fine, Aidan, really. It's only just hit me now. And it's because we are on the same strip of road and it's dark."

I turned around, and headlights burned into my eyes as a car sped up close to us. I started to shake.

Aidan turned to see what had made me so tense. When the vehicle overtook us, he took a deep breath, and my body slumped into his.

He stroked me gently, drawing apprehension out of my muscles. "Baby, maybe you should see someone. I could make an appointment with Kieren. He's helped me plenty."

I exhaled a shaky breath. "No. Really, I'm fine. It just brought it all back." He drew me in tight. "And with you holding me, Aidan, I could face a seven-headed monster spewing out fire, and I'd still feel safe."

Aidan sniffed. "You didn't happen to eat any of Simon's cookies, did you?"

I giggled. "No. I didn't. Tabitha did, and she was pretty giggly there for a while."

He buried his nose into my hair and kissed me. "While I'm around, princess, no harm will ever come to you. I'd kill for you."

"I hope that won't be necessary because I couldn't imagine my life without you, Aidan. And I'd hate to have to visit you in jail."

"You'll never have to do that, darling. We're safe. I've seen to that."

I was relieved when the big iron fortress opened up and swallowed us back into the safety of my beautiful stately home. That hard, metallic yawn was music to my ears.

Aidan had made a good point. I probably needed to see someone, because I found myself dripping in cold sweat after that ride home. It hadn't happened before. But then I hadn't been out in a car at night since the car chase incident. Like some creepy phantom streaking its icy presence on my skin, the mystery of who was behind it continued to haunt me.

James jumped out and opened the doors for us.

"Thanks, man," said Aidan, stretching his long legs out. "Where's Linus, I wonder?" He looked at James, who shook his head.

Aidan put his arm around me. The cool air shivered through me. "Come on. Let's get you in." He turned to James. "We'll see you in the morning. I've got an early flight."

"Sure thing, Aidan." James turned to me and smiled. "Sleep well."

"Thanks for everything, James," I replied.

• • • ● • ● • • • •

IT FELT SO WONDERFUL to be on my favorite sofa, wearing a cozy sweater and comfy leggings, watching TV.

Aidan sat at his desk, getting his itinerary together for the morning. Every now and then, he'd glance up at me with his large blue eyes glistening with tenderness. His delectably sculptured lips curved up at one end, the promise of which set off an electrical charge through me.

Rocket was at his feet, snoozing.

I stretched out like a lazy cat. *Could life get any better?*

"I'll be there in a minute, baby," said Aidan.

"It's okay. Take your time. I'm just really happy to be home."

"You look good enough to eat, baby. I love seeing you without make-up and your hair down. And what's underneath that sweater, I wonder?"

"Not much." I giggled.

He stood up and came toward me, his stride elegant but purposeful.

"I thought you were busy," I said, looking up at him.

"It can wait." He lowered down to his knee, and his hands went exploring beneath my sweater. He groaned as he caressed my breasts. "Are you cold? Let's put the heat on so that I can take this off."

"I'm not cold now," I murmured.

Just as Aidan lifted my sweater, Rocket barked and began to growl and his fur stood up. My breath hitched. I'd never seen him behave like that before.

Aidan's eyebrows knitted. He sprang up. "What is it, buddy?"

Rocket ran to the door, continuing to growl. He made such a loud commotion, and there was no way to calm him. Aidan stepped out onto the balcony in order to survey the grounds.

"Maybe there's a cat out there," I called out.

Aidan's furrowed brow told me otherwise, as my teeth dug into my lip. "It's not a cat. Rocket never does this unless…" He opened a drawer and took out a gun.

"Unless?" quivered out of my throat.

Aidan grabbed my phone and handed it to me. "Go into the bathroom and lock the door."

"Aidan, what is it?"

"Just do it, Clarissa, now." His voice resonated in commando style.

Rocket was barking so loudly, it was hard to think, let alone ask questions.

Aidan slid a magazine into his gun. I started to shake with fear. I'd never seen a gun, let alone watch someone preparing one for use. Aidan led me by the arm to the bathroom.

He looked at me, his mouth tight. Aidan's steely focus softened a little when he noticed me trembling. "It's probably nothing, my love. Just go in there and lock the door. If I haven't come back in five minutes, call 911. Okay?"

"Aidan…"

After he shut the door, I locked it, just as instructed.

I hugged my body as my teeth chattered. I told myself that it was probably a false alarm and that Rocket was barking at a rat in the house or something. It was the "or something" that made my legs turn into jelly.

I slid against the wall and sat on the bathroom floor. I held my head in fear. After a pep talk from a cool, calm, and collected part of my brain, telling me to get a grip, I stood up and placed my ear to the door.

Rocket's bark was now in the distance. The fact he was still causing a ruckus didn't help. My jaw remained tight.

I stared at my phone, wondering if it had been five minutes yet.

CHAPTER TWELVE

AIDAN

I'D NEVER SEEN ROCKET that agitated before. He charged on ahead, as I descended the stairs. Once I got to the ground floor, I stood tight to the wall. I'd been trained to do this. But in the dark of night, amidst billionaire's comfort, it was somewhat different from what I'd experienced out in the fields during combat.

Rocket turned the corner into the main salon. He let out an almighty growl. He'd come across the felon. Of that, I was certain.

Just as I was about to move into the dark room, gunfire rang through the air. Within a second, Rocket let out a blood-curdling squeal and fell to the ground.

A noxious cocktail of rage, pain, fear, and desperation thundered through me, a fury of emotion as blood rumbled through me. My muscles were tight and battle-ready as I charged forward with arms extended and my finger, steadier than the rest of me, positioned on the trigger.

I turned the corner and immediately aimed at the shadow before me. Seconds became valuable. Just as my crooked finger pulled the trigger, a bullet flew past me. My reflexes heightened in response as I let off a round from my semi-automatic gun. I hit the target, and he thudded to the ground.

Another bullet pierced the dark air. Even though it felt as if a blade had sliced along my bicep, I didn't feel much. Adrenaline had robbed me of sensation.

When I noticed him moving, I fired another shot, and he fell back.

I turned on the light.

There in a pool of blood lay John Howard. In shock, I remained frozen before quickly snapping out of it.

I bent down to Rocket. When I felt his little heart beating against my hand, I sighed loudly. But he was in pain. The poor creature's whimpering made my eyes cloud with tears.

I then went to Howard's inert body and felt his carotid artery. It was lifeless. The corpse's ugly eyes reflected the evil sonofabitch as I'd always remembered him.

Clarissa came running down the stairs. "Aidan!"

"Have you called 911?"

"Yes, but they can't get in."

"Ah... shit. Where the fuck's Linus?"

I quickly turned the light off. I didn't want Clarissa to see the body. "Don't come any closer," I said.

She stared down at my arm, which was bleeding. "But you're wounded, Aidan." She looked down and saw Rocket whimpering. She held her mouth and fell to her knees. "Rocket."

"He's been shot in the leg," I said, my voice thick with a threatening sob. "I'll run out and let them in. Just stay here, and comfort Rocket. Don't turn the light on. Promise me."

I left her and raced out.

When I arrived at the control room, there was still no sign of Linus. On the security screen, I saw the police waiting at the gate, and the ambulance had just arrived behind them. I hoped I could convince them to look at Rocket. That was my main concern at that moment, getting my dog to a vet.

I hit the switch to open the iron gates.

I stood waiting for them as they drove toward me.

When the police stepped out of their vehicle, they saw me holding my wound. My shirtsleeve was soaked in blood.

"You've been shot," said the officer.

"I have. He's in there. Dead, I think. I knew him. My dog's been shot. I need to get him to a vet."

The young cop said, "You look like you need a hospital too."

"Don't worry about me. It's only a flesh wound. You need to go inside and deal with the body. My fiancée's still in there with my dog. She'll be frightened. Don't let her see the body."

"Sure," he said. "You can wait here and get your wound seen to."

"No, I want to come with you," I said.

The ambulance pulled up, and while one policeman went up the path to the house, the other insisted I remain there to have my wound looked at.

The paramedic jumped out with a bag and approached me. He tried to get a close look, but I moved away.

"My dog, please," I pleaded, and before he could do anything I'd turned toward the house. He could do little but follow me. "Bring your bag of tricks. My dog needs seeing to, now."

Clarissa ran to me. "Aidan."

I ripped my sleeve and tied it around my wound. "Clarissa, please go upstairs and wait."

But she remained stubbornly put.

The policeman approached me. "I believe you knew the victim?"

"Yeah, John Howard, recently let out of jail. He killed his wife, who I knew."

He nodded.

I was too focused on Rocket. After the paramedic injected him, I asked, "Is he going to be all right?"

"I've given him some morphine. It's not my area of expertise, you realize, but at least I can bandage him up until the vet arrives."

I squeezed Clarissa's hand and let out a tight breath.

"Rocket has been seen to. Now you have to, Aidan," she urged.

The paramedic looked at me and nodded in agreement. I could do little but agree, as the policeman and Clarissa accompanied me back to the ambulance.

"I'll take a statement from you in the morning," said the policeman. "I can see it was self-defense. But we will still have to go through due process. We've sent for the forensic team. Nothing must be moved or touched. You haven't tampered with anything, I trust?"

I shook my head. "Whatever you have to do, Officer. Only try to clear it away as soon as possible."

"You're lucky there's no bullet. It scraped past you," said the paramedic.

"Then bandage me up here. I need to find my security guard."

The police officer looked at me. "Has he gone missing?"

"Yes." I grimaced after the paramedic sprayed something on my wound.

"It may hurt," he said.

"I've felt worse." I looked at Clarissa, who watched on. Her wide eyes, glassy with fear. I just wanted to take her and hold her. "Come here, sweetheart."

She came by my side. I held her hand as the paramedic bandaged my wound.

"You're not in pain?" she asked.

"It's not that bad. I'm just worried about Rocket."

I heard a vehicle entering the estate and saw that it was the emergency home vet service. "They're here. Thank God."

When the vehicle pulled up, Clarissa said, "Don't worry, Aidan. Leave it to me. I'll take him to Rocket."

I kissed her. "I love you."

She looked deep into my eyes. Her wide eyes glistened with tears. "I love you too."

She was about to step away and I pulled her back. "I'm sorry to do this to you, baby."

Her lips twitched into a faint smile.

After the police left and Rocket had been taken away to the animal hospital, I went back upstairs. My arm was bandaged, and I was as restless as they come, pacing about as if a monster had taken possession of me.

Poor Clarissa sat there silently, watching.

"I'm going to look for Linus. He's got to be here somewhere. His car's there."

"But what if something happened to him?" asked Clarissa in a small quivering voice.

"Then that will explain it," I replied.

Driven by the need for answers, fury fired me along. All I could think of was Rocket. I prayed he would survive. The vet had given me cause for hope when he said that the creature's vital organs were safe.

A tear dropped on my cheek. I loved my dog. He was the hero of the moment. He'd saved us. If he hadn't alerted us, something more sinister could have happened, considering the door to our private quarters had been unlocked. There was no doubt in my mind that Howard had been on his way up.

I entered the kitchen. There was nobody around, so I stepped outside into the courtyard. I could see Susana's room was lit. That seemed to be the only sign of life. Will was out for the night, and Roland spent his weekends away.

The thought of knocking on Susana's door made me cringe. She was such a flirt, and I wasn't in the mood for her sleazy advances.

A weird feeling suddenly hit me. What if Linus was there?

I stood by the door and was about to knock when I heard loud moans and groans. Noticing that the curtain was slightly open, I peeked in. My veins froze. I'd found Linus. His big, bulky frame was on his knees with his head buried between Susana's legs. She was moaning with her head tossed back. Fuck.

Just as she was screaming through an orgasm, I knocked. There was a pause, then I heard some shuffling.

"Who is it?" she asked.

I leaned against the door. "Aidan." My voice rang with authority.

Holding a skimpy towel that barely did the job, Susana poked her head out. "Hi. I'd invite you in, but..."

"I'm here for Linus."

"Oh?" she said. "I'm not sure..."

I interjected, "I know he's in there, Susana." I pushed the door open, and she stumbled back.

As I barged in, bare-chested Linus sprang to his feet while doing up the zipper of his pants.

He looked at my arm. "Shit. What happened to you?"

"I'll tell you what happened to me. I was shot. And so was Rocket. And I tell you what. If he dies..." I pointed my finger in his face.

His face crumpled in dismay. "Shit."

"Where the fuck, were you?" I shouted. Seeing this strong, powerful man cowering before me made my knuckles whiten from fury.

"I didn't think you were going to be back until late, and I..."

"You have to be at your fucking post regardless of whether I'm in or out. You know the score. That's why I pay you a truckload of money. To keep us safe. And to keep the estate watched over."

I had to squeeze every ounce of control because I wanted to crush my fist down on his sweaty face. I bit my lip, using every ounce of willpower I could muster.

While Linus whimpered some lame excuse, I directed my focus on Susana, who stood there half-naked. I noted a gleam in her eye that nearly made me convulse. She was enjoying herself.

Clarissa had been right about her all along. She was gutter material. I only kept her there because of Will.

"Go and put some fucking clothes on, will you? In the morning, you're out. I don't want to see your loose ass around here ever again."

As she crept off, I yelled out behind her, "I thought you were fucking Will."

Linus stared down at his feet. "Aidan, I'm sorry, man. She, you know..."

"She seduced you. Yes. I get it. We could have been killed. Instead, I've got blood on my hands. I had to kill a man because you couldn't keep your cock inside your pants."

"You shot the intruder?" Linus asked.

"Yeah, the fucker's dead. It was either him or those I loved." I combed my hair back with my wet palm. A realization had just hit me. This was the second man I'd killed in my life, and despite hating the sonofabitch, it left me gasping for air.

A bitter taste landed at the back of my throat a remnant of the churning bile being whipped up in my belly.

Susana stepped out and looked at me, her face pale and drawn. "He's dead?"

I frowned and cast a quick glance at Linus, who was equally puzzled by her reaction. My eyes narrowed. "Why should that concern you?"

A tear dropped on her cheek.

I charged toward her and grabbed her arm. "You fucking knew him, didn't you? This was all your doing?" I shouted so loudly she winced. Her expression switched from sad to haughty in one beat.

She spat in my face. I pushed her, and she fell to the ground on her ass.

Linus stood between us. "Aidan."

"I'm not going to hit her. That would feed her scheme to bring me down.

Linus helped her up. His face was cold. "You lured me, you bitch." Now it was his turn to vent rage. He pushed her onto the sofa. "Stay still."

Susana leaned over to the drawer. Linus grabbed her arm. "Don't you even think about it."

He looked in the drawer and brought out a pistol. "Now what have we here?" Linus passed it to me.

"Are you related to John Howard?" I asked, standing over her.

"He's my father."

My eyes stretched wide. "You're Susie, Jacqui's daughter?"

"Yes. She was my mother. You murdered her."

"I did no such fucking thing. Your father murdered her."

"Only because you made her unfaithful," she shot back.

"She seduced me, Susie. And in any case, your father was beating her to a pulp every night."

"It was none of your business. My father loved my mother!" she cried.

I looked at Linus. "Call the cops. She's an accomplice."

"If you get me arrested, I'll sell this story to the papers."

"Call the cops, Linus."

He took out his phone. She touched my arm. "No. Please. Don't. I'll go. I won't say anything. I promise."

I shook her off. "I don't believe you. You turned yourself into a honey-trap so that those I love..." My voice strained it was so thick with emotion. "You're lucky nothing happened to Clarissa."

"I would've popped a champagne cork if that had happened," she said, reverting to nasty defiance.

My fists clenched, pumped and ready. I had to fight every little sinew in my body. I would never hit a woman. But that was torture. Her dark, evil expression sent cold sweat dripping down my back. Like father, like daughter.

"What?"

She stood there with her hands on her hips, willing me on to attack her. "You heard me."

"You fucking whore," I spat with the fury of a punch.

I turned to Linus. "Call the cops."

He tapped the number into his phone.

She went to run, but I grabbed her in time. "Tie her down first."

Linus said, "With pleasure."

She writhed about like a wild cat as Linus wound sticky tape around her wrists and legs.

"Put some on that dirty mouth," I said.

After I was no longer needed, I headed out. Before leaving, I turned and sniggered darkly in her face. "Rot in hell."

CHAPTER THIRTEEN

CLARISSA

WHILE AIDAN WAS AWAY, I paced about the room. He took longer than my nerves could handle.

I lost count of the number of times I peered out from the balcony and onto the grounds. To say I was spooked was an understatement of how I really felt. My heart leaped at every little rustle.

Some good news had arrived while Aidan was out. Although I was not in the habit of reading his messages, I read the message from the vet advising that Rocket was doing well. I sighed loudly. My chest, which had been tied in knots, unraveled a little.

I forgot I'd locked the door so that when the handle turned and a knock followed, I jumped out of my skin.

"It's me." Aidan's voice echoed in the hallway.

I ran and opened it. "Aidan." I fell into his arms. "Rocket's going to be fine."

He pulled his head back, and his face brightened. "Really? They called?"

I nodded. "Sorry for looking at your phone, but I sensed it might've been about Rocket. I was desperate to know."

"It's okay, princess. I don't mind you looking at my phone. I have nothing to hide from you. I've got to go back downstairs to the police."

"The police? Again?"

Looking exhausted, he rubbed his neck. I noted the same haunted expression I'd seen earlier. He exhaled a deep breath. "I found Linus with Susana."

I gasped. "I had a feeling that was where he was."

Aidan studied me with a puzzled frown.

"I've seen them together before."

"And you never thought to tell me?" His annoyance scraped my heart.

"I forgot. So much was going on, and I…" My eyes pooled with tears. I couldn't handle all this drama. I wished my father had returned.

Aidan's eyes softened. "I'm sorry, angel. It's been a crazy night." He came to me and held me. I tried to quell the maelstrom brewing but couldn't, and tears poured down my cheeks as my body convulsed with sobs.

Aidan held me for a moment when his phone pinged.

I pulled away. "I'm detaining you."

"No, you're not. You're everything. You come first. Always." Aidan's eyes shone with sincerity.

He walked to his phone and read the message. "I've got to go downstairs. I'll be back soon."

Aidan didn't return until early morning. When he came home, he fell onto the bed. I undid his shoes and removed his clothes. He mumbled something about having to call off his trip to New York then fell into a deep sleep.

It wasn't until the afternoon when Aidan surfaced. I busied myself in the office, dealing with the needs of the charities and paying bills. It was a full-time affair. I appreciated just how much Greta did. Nevertheless, the distraction was a godsend.

Chris had called that morning. As usual, he sounded half asleep when he asked about supplies, especially since the student numbers were growing. I told him I'd drop in the following day.

Aidan came and found me. He leaned against the door. Despite the stress of the night before etched on his beautiful face, he still mustered a sweet smile.

"Hey, angel. What are you up to?"

I went over and held him.

"Ah, that feels better," he crooned.

"I had to pay a few bills for the refuges, and Chris needs more supplies. The program's going really well again."

Aidan nodded reflectively. "Good." He sighed. "Come and have a coffee with me."

It was weird, but this was the first time in the four months that I'd been seeing Aidan that we hadn't made love. Aidan put his arm around my waist and drew me so close I could feel his bulging thigh muscles against my hip.

"I'm glad you're with me, Clarissa. Today would've felt bleak otherwise."

I stopped walking and turned. "Aidan, you will tell me what happened?"

Aidan nodded.

I nearly spilled the coffee from my cup when learning that Susana was actually John Howard's daughter. Discovering that, along with her evil father, she'd plotted to kill Aidan, left me speechless.

"You warned me about her." Aidan stroked my hand.

"I saw her with Linus the same night I was in the car chase."

Aidan's brow wrinkled. "Why didn't you tell me?"

"It slipped my mind. So much was going on." My voice tightened. "Do you think that they were involved in the car chase?"

Aidan shook his head.

"But how do you know that?"

"Because yesterday I got word that a body had washed up."

My eyes stretched wide. "And you didn't think to tell me?"

"Hell, Clarissa, so much has happened in the past twenty-four hours. To be honest, I forgot."

Aidan's eyes, screaming for mercy, did little to quell my unrest.

I stood up. "This all too much for me. I don't know if I can handle it. You never tell me anything. You're secretive to a fault."

My legs turned to concrete. I remained there wanting to scream. I couldn't figure what made me angrier, the fact Aidan kept me in the dark, or at having discovered that I'd inadvertently killed someone.

Aidan grabbed my hand. "What do you mean? You're not leaving me, are you?"

Frozen on the spot, I fell deeply into his dark gaze, as an aching gap stretched between us.

Aidan's pleading stare touched me profoundly, all the way to my soul.

I wanted to run. I wanted to go to the cottage and bury my head in a book or anything that would help me forget everything. I wasn't good at drama. Especially with the threat of revenge clinging to every fixture of our lives.

His eyes glistened with a watery film. Oh my, Aidan was about to break. He'd once admitted to me that he'd never been able to cry. But as I drowned in his despair, I sensed something deep within him was about to erupt.

My heart melted with pity, love, and helplessness.

"Aidan, no... I couldn't..."

He lowered his head into his hands as if he'd been injured.

"Aidan, I'm not leaving. I'm just frightened that someone will harm you. Harm us."

His intense gaze ate me up. His eyes had gone such an impossible shade of blue they swallowed my soul. A tear slid down his cheek.

I held him as a mother would a son.

Somehow, his weakness had become my strength. Eventually, I whispered, "Aidan, the very devil could enter this house, and I'd still remain with you."

He unraveled from my arms and stroked my cheek. His lips twitched into a faint smile.

"Come on, angel. Let's go for a walk."

The air packed a punch. I felt instantly revived.

There was something eminently healing about a sea breeze. Its energy flowed through my veins. Walking by my side, Aidan remained quiet as he held me tight. It was comfortable silence. I read somewhere that the test of true love was that a couple could remain silent and still feel loved. We had that. His body pressed gently against mine, felt so warm and reassuring that my spirit had been suddenly restored.

As we strolled along the cobbled path back to the estate, in the distance, we saw Rocket sitting placidly on the lawn with Roland.

The faithful creature hobbled over to us, his tail wagging, his big brown eyes filled with love and gratitude. My heart melted at the sight of him. Aidan lavished him with pats and hugs. That was despite Rocket's wound being bandaged and the vet's instruction to avoid excitement.

It was a hero's welcome, nevertheless. Rocket had been rewarded with a nice big juicy bone. The handsome mutt looked up at us with his big brown eyes, thanking us for saving his life.

"You're the hero, buddy. If it weren't for you, God knows what might have happened," said Aidan, letting Rocket show his slobbering affection by licking his face and hands.

Tears rolled down my cheeks. What a pretty sight they made, man and dog sharing in the joy of being together.

Aidan looked up at me. "Our boy's home and life's good again."

Before leaving Rocket to devour his bone, Aidan instructed Roland to keep an eye on the canine and to not allow him to climb the stairs until his wound had healed.

After dinner, Aidan and I settled on the sofa and watched something mindless on TV. Despite our having laid to rest the unease that had taken hostage of our fairy-tale existence, there was still one prickly subject that needed seeing to.

"Aidan, tell me about the body that washed up."

He took a deep breath. "He's been identified as a hitman. The police have no doubt that he was the one driving the car."

"Are they sure? I mean, how can they tell he was the driver?"

"It was a rental car. And the ID they found on him was the same as the one registered with the rental company."

"I suppose that confirms it, then." I paused to contemplate. "Why didn't he seek help?"

"Good question. I imagine he crawled out and might have stumbled down the rocks into the sea. Anything like that's plausible."

I grimaced.

"Baby, don't put yourself through this. Let me deal with it. I don't want to fill that pretty head of yours with ugly images."

"I need to know, Aidan. It's haunting me, to be honest. I feel like I killed him. I did, really—didn't I?"

Aidan faced me squarely. "Far from it. It was either you or him. His record's soaked in blood. You did society a favor."

"You make me sound like a vigilante."

"In this game of survival, the best outcome is the one where the good guy or girl comes out on top. And you, baby, were amazing. Apart from being left speechless by your beauty that just grows each time I look at you, words cannot explain how much I admire you for how you handled that situation. You were brave and demonstrated presence of mind. In the Forces, they trained that into us. But not many had that, really. Where most would've freaked out, you, baby, kicked ass. And thank God, because if anything had happened to you..."

My body warmed, and I fell into Aidan's reassuring hold. Vanity pushed away any misgivings. I loved hearing that every time he looked at me, I grew more beautiful. Funny thing about that...every time I viewed Aidan's handsome face and scrumptious body the same thing happened to me.

"Then who could have hired him? We now know it wasn't Bryce. Could it have been John Howard?"

Aidan shook his head. "I don't think it was. Brutes like him get off on pain in their victims' eyes and cries for mercy."

I shivered.

"Sorry, baby. Am I being too gory?"

"No, you're not. I'm not a child, you know." My tone was prickly.

"You're right. I keep forgetting how strong you are, Clarissa. Your big, beautiful eyes and sensitivity make me want to protect you from the ugliness of the world. I know this sounds a little uncouth. But at times I feel like a father to you."

"Mm... that reminds me of something I read once," I said.

"What was that?"

"That in an ideal relationship, the man should be like a father, brother, and son, and the woman, a mother, sister, and daughter."

Aidan considered this for a moment. "That makes sense, a protector, a friend, and someone who needs you."

"I think that sounds healthy. Don't you?" I asked.

He nodded slowly. A little twinkle in his eyes flickered playfully. "Does that mean I'm being incestuous?" His hand slid up my thigh and traveled under my skirt all the delicious way up. "Oh, baby, you're not wearing panties."

I giggled. I thought it was high time we played. I told myself that all the drama that had consumed our beautiful existence needed to be buried by a good session of heavy lovemaking. Therefore, I made sure I removed my panties before Aidan joined me.

"Mm... your pretty little pussy has been neglected. And it's oh so delectable."

His finger caressed my bud with a perfect, soft touch, then ramping up the heat, two fingers entered, making my fiery nerve endings send electrifying tingles through me. He undid the buttons of my blouse and found my breasts hungering for his attention.

I unzipped his jeans and freed him. His thick, heavy cock pulsed frantically in my hand, while Aidan's lips took to my nipples with the avidity of one starved.

He ripped off my clothes. "Open your legs, princess. Let me look at that pretty pink pussy before I ravish it."

Mm... what was a girl to do? I opened wide while gazing into his lust-filled eyes.

He held his heavy cock and positioned it. As the slick, thick head entered, I moaned through the intense stretch of it filling me with that indescribable pleasurable ache that made my heart bang fiercely against my chest. He pushed his pelvis against mine, every delicious inch buried deeply into me, and a loud agonized growl left his parted lips.

CHAPTER FOURTEEN

I DROPPED INTO THE VHC to see how things were going in the world of art making. Although Roy had set up his own studio, he still attended the classes for Chris's expert guidance and to hang out with his friends.

I stood in the room laden with canvases, moving from image to image. There was lots of variety, from contemporary abstract art to vases of flowers, portraits, landscapes, and images of pets.

It was inspiring being there. Just like the first time I walked into that room to observe the program in full flight, I was struck by how fruitful Aidan's scheme had been. Most of the students who had come bearing heavy scars were at that moment, in my eyes, at least, transformed. I could tell by their concentrated attention that they were absorbed in what they were doing. I could see that they'd invested their heart and soul into their creations.

Chris was instructing a woman on how to mix color and apply it with a palette knife.

He glanced up and asked me, "What do you think?"

I studied the self-portrait rendered in crude brush and palette knife strokes, reminiscent of Van Gogh.

"It's fantastic." I smiled at the artist. She gazed up at me with a shy smile of gratitude.

"Chris, the work is mind-boggling. You're really bringing the best out of students."

He rubbed his messy blond hair, making it stick up all over the place. He really looked as if he'd rolled out of bed and dressed in the dark. But then, that was Chris. He had that grunge thing happening. Not that I believed he designed it that way. That concept would have been abhorrent to someone as original as Chris. But he was a type. Just as we all were.

"I can't say it's my doing, Clarissa."

"You're being too modest," I countered, glancing up at the woman whose work we were studying.

She nodded in agreement with me.

"Chris is a grumpy so-and-so," she said with a chuckle. "But he's brought my markings to life. That's for sure."

"They're more than markings. It's a terrific self-portrait," I said.

"There are some great pieces," said Chris, directing me to his office. "I especially like some of the abstract-expressionist ones. Did you see Mary's canvas?"

"I did. It's very original and fashionable at the same time."

"My thoughts exactly. Speaking of which, have you set a date for the next auction?" He gestured with his arm for me to enter his office.

"I asked Aidan, and he thought we could run one in a month's time. I will have to send out the invites and market it. That shouldn't be hard. I've been swamped with requests for placement on the mailing list."

Chris nodded. His lips formed a lazy smile. I was sure he'd been up all night. His face had that pale-and-haggard look about it.

"Yep, the program has had good press, all right. You're a talented publicist, Clarissa Moone."

"I've done very little. I just got in touch with some art publications and websites and plugged the philanthropic element." I smiled. I was feeling lighter than I should have, considering what had transpired that week.

Aidan had devoured me good and proper, and I was high on post-orgasmic endorphins. In fact, like Chris, I was permanently high. In my case, sex being the drug.

As I studied Chris, I saw something in his heavy blue eyes that made me feel pity and affection at the same time. He'd always inspired that in me. I never knew I could like someone who was a drug addict. If anything, it highlighted how closed-minded society was about these things.

"How have you been?" I asked, taking the cup of coffee he handed me.

He held up a bottle of bourbon and dropped some into his coffee. "Do you want some?"

I shook my head.

After he took a sip his focus returned to me. "I've been okay, I suppose. You know me."

"I don't know you, Chris, that well. All I know is that you're seriously talented and that I worry about you."

His head pushed back sharply. "You worry about me?"

"Yeah, I do. I know you're into shooting heroin, and I fear that we'll find you on the floor one day."

"Ah... you don't want to clean up after a junkie. That's understandable. It's not pretty." His tone was dry and unaffected.

"No, that's not what I meant. Both Aidan and I respect you. We like you as a person. Not just as an artist."

He raised his eyebrows and drew a tight smile. "But you hardly know me. I could be an evil motherfucker, for all you know."

"Well, if you are, you're a talented evil motherfucker."

He laughed with a croaky husk while lighting a cigarette. "Even when you talk dirty, Clarissa Moone, you make it sound sweet. Your little witchy face glows delightfully as if you've entered a den of sin."

"I'm not that innocent, you know."

His eyes glowed playfully. "I know. I've watched how you gaze salaciously at Aidan, devouring him with those witchy eyes of yours."

My face heated. "Have I been that obvious?"

"Uh-huh."

"But seriously, Chris. Is there anything we can do? You know, rehab? I'd be happy to pay."

"You're too generous." He snorted. "I'm a man born out of my time. I'm doing a Thomas De Quincey."

"But you're romanticizing it. Even De Quincey admitted to the drug's hellish grip on his life."

"I don't know what impresses me more, the fact you've read De Quincey, or that you care about my well-being," he said with a dismissive smirk.

"I've read heaps of books in my short life."

"Then you will appreciate that I feel like a ghost passing through life. That it's only when I paint that I escape something that seems inescapable. And that living in this technological, plastic world fills my waking hours with the need to drift about with my eyes half-closed."

"For an artist whose line is so confident and pure and color palette that, although reckless, is eye-catching and just right, you don't strike me as someone who walks about with his eyes closed."

"I couldn't find those curves or juxtapose color and break every rule nature has thrown at us if I didn't walk around with my eyes half shut. Can't you see that? Reality is so beige, square, rectangular shapes that use asymmetry as if it's making some fucking bold statement for originality. That does my head in. And there's all the fucking plastic everywhere."

I had to laugh. His eyes had gone all fiery and wide for the first time.

"We don't have to go down the path of technology. There are books, art, and beauty."

"Mm... beauty you say?"

"Well, yes. Europe, for instance, is filled with magnificence. It's like one big glorious museum."

"Even that is too sugary sweet for me. I like grungy, dark matter. Beauty is a subjective concept, Clarissa. I find old dilapidated buildings beautiful. I find old broken-down women beautiful, more so than the plastic chicks going around showing off their fake tits and butt implants. Fuck me, can someone shoot the dude who came up with that fucking invention."

I had to giggle at his acerbic tone. "I am also born out of my time. I have a penchant for all things 1960s."

He stared at my polka-dot shift and white boots. "I've noticed." His face went serious. "Clarissa, you're one of a kind, as is Aidan. His generosity and appreciation for art resonate with the Renaissance sensibility. While you, pretty little witch, are clever, talented and true to your soul. You're so blissfully ethereal, I can imagine you floating through the air."

I laughed. I loved hearing myself described like that, and Aidan as a Renaissance man—a kind of sweet version of Medici without being underhanded and murderous.

"Speaking of all things plastic, are you still seeing Jessica?"

"Meow..." Chris clawed his fingers. His eyes twinkled with amusement. "I'm not seeing her as such. But she has this annoying tendency to drop in wearing very little under her designer coats. And she gives good head, so I overlook the fact that none of her is real."

I laughed again. "Chris, you're one of a kind. And we don't want to lose you. Life would be dull without you."

"Bullshit. I'm a tiny dot in the whole scheme of things." His face cracked into a lopsided grin. "Still, it's nice to hear your words of encouragement. And hey, there's no need to worry about me. I'm not drugging out as much as I used to. I'm more of a dabbler these days."

"That gives me hope, Chris."

CHAPTER FIFTEEN

TABITHA BOUNCED ALONG, WITH her arm linked in mine. Aidan had gone ahead to chat with his pilot.

"I can't believe we're about to go to New York together, and in a private plane."

Not as upbeat as Tabitha, I felt a tiny sizzle of anxiety threatening my inner peace and breakfast. I was a nervous flyer, and my tight smile said it all.

"Don't be scared, Clary. We'll just sink back a few champagnes, and it will be all good."

As always, Tabitha's excitement was contagious, helping push any fear to the back of my mind.

I cast my eyes at my handsome husband-to-be. He stood there with those big arms crossed. His beige chinos showed off that firm butt that, only hours earlier, I'd grasped onto while supping on his thick cock in the shower.

After we boarded the private jet, we made our way into the lounge area. Decked out in red leather, the cabin looked inviting and unexpectedly spacious. Tabitha fell into one of the chairs and moved her head about like a restless child. "This is incredible. One could live in this."

"Maybe *you* could."

Her face broke into a sympathetic smile. "Don't worry. You'll have Aidan holding your hand."

"Yeah, I guess it will be okay."

Aidan came in and sat next to me. I felt better already. "Are you okay?"

"Now that you're here, I am."

He smiled.

A red-haired stewardess came out and asked us if we wished for refreshment. Tabitha went for the champagne, while I settled for a juice.

I must have squeezed the blood out of Aidan's hand as the plane bounced up and down before its wheels thudded onto the ground.

Aidan turned and looked at me. "We're safe, baby."

I looked up at him, expelling a long, sharp breath. "It's the takeoff and the landing that I hate. Not to mention the turbulence."

His eyes reflected understanding. "I was the same, princess. But the Forces ironed that out of me by making me jump from planes."

I shivered. "Skydiving—now that would really be a hellish experience."

Tabitha took her earplugs out. "What's hellish?"

"Jumping out of a plane."

Aidan smiled. "You won't have to do that today. We can walk out."

I giggled and kissed him on the cheek.

When we were walking along the tarmac, I said, "I've never really asked you about your army days and training. It sounds like an adventure."

"Mm... adventure is a nice way of putting it. Let's just say it made me what I am today."

"Then it was miraculous. Because you're miraculous, Aidan," I said, wrapping my arm around his waist.

He smiled. "And you, baby, are looking sexy as hell in that little dress and those boots."

I touched my dress with pride. "I love this little Mondrian dress that my mother bought on Carnaby Street."

"With those scrumptious shapely legs, you wear it well. It's eccentric. But I love it with the white boots. Reminds me of something 99 wore."

I giggled at Aidan's reference to *Get Smart*. That was another thing we shared, a deep affection for 1960s television shows.

"Aidan, thanks for letting Tabitha come with us."

He played with my braid. "I'm going to be pretty flat out during the days. I didn't like the idea of you roaming the streets alone."

"What? You thought Tabitha would make a good chaperone?"

Aidan grinned at my incredulous smirk. "Not exactly. And it is risky considering her tendency to collect men everywhere she goes. But I figured there was little trouble you could get into shopping."

"You're so generous. Tabitha will go nuts in the shops."

He shrugged. "As long as you go nuts as well."

I stroked his white linen shirt. His face was clean-shaven for a change. Not that I minded his five o'clock shadow scraping along my thigh.

An older man waited by a black Mercedes.

"Hello, Aidan. Welcome back."

"Mike, good to see you. How's your daughter?"

"She's much better. Thank you, Aidan. It meant everything. If there's ever anything I can do."

"This is my fiancée, Clarissa, and Tabitha, a friend," said Aidan.

We both smiled and greeted him.

By the way Mike looked at me, I could tell Aidan had told him about me.

He held out his hand. "Pleased to meet you at last. I've heard much about you."

"Mike will be your driver. He'll take you wherever you want to go," said Aidan.

Tabitha sat quietly, but I could see her face was alive with excitement.

The closer we got to the busy city, the thicker the traffic became. There were cars everywhere, making it a gridlock as we remained idling.

It was as if we were at a theme park. Tabitha kept tapping my arm and pointing to designer shops and all the famous sites that we'd only ever seen on TV. We'd never been out of LA, which heightened the experience more so.

As we drove down the famous Fifth Avenue, Tabitha screamed with glee when we passed Dolce and Gabbana, especially after she discovered we were going to be staying close by.

I was more taken with Tiffany's. "Hey, look, Tabs." I pointed to the famous locale. "Should we have breakfast there?"

Aidan looked at me. "It's a jewelry store, princess."

I giggled. *Breakfast at Tiffany's.* You know, the movie."

He nodded. "Ah... of course."

Tabitha chimed in, "If you turn up in one of your little dresses, black, of course, and we tease your hair up into a French roll, then you could almost pull it off. Although we'll have to strap down those big boobs of yours. Audrey was rather flat-chested."

"You'll do no such thing," said Aidan, drawing me close. He lowered his voice. "I want them free and in my mouth by day's end."

I laughed.

Tabitha shook her head. "You two are in heat."

"Speaking of which, why didn't Grant come along?" I asked.

"He's got a gig tonight," replied Tabitha. "He also has an aversion to New York for some reason."

"Grant's Venice, through and through, inside out," said Aidan.

"I've noticed," said Tabitha dryly.

We pulled up at the curb, and as I looked up, I stared at the sky-hugging heritage building. "Is this where we're staying?" I asked, stepping onto the pavement.

Aidan said, "Yes, all the way up. We're at the top."

"Oh God," said Tabitha, turning about on the pavement. She didn't know where to look. There was so much going on. People moved along with purposeful steps, eyes pitched ahead, on a mission. We had to keep dodging them.

In fact, infinite streams of people and dogs cluttered the pavement. I couldn't believe how many canines there were. I peered across the wide road to Central Park, which was where I imagined they'd been for their daily walk.

My eyes remained fixed on the abundance of green manicured trees that made for a relaxing juxtaposition to all the concrete everywhere.

"Central Park," I crooned. "I finally get to see it."

"Later on, today, we'll take a walk, angel," said Aidan.

"I would love that." Bubbles of anticipation, which had started from the moment I saw Tiffany's shivered through me. Tabitha's contagious elation only adding to it.

The marble floor echoed under our feet as we made our way to the elevator.

"I feel like I'm in a movie," I said.

"Me, too," said Tabitha.

Aidan's lips curled into a faint smile. He was just happy to see me content. We'd been through much in recent times. For Aidan, this trip was about me letting my hair down and enjoying myself.

Tabitha and I ran around the penthouse suite, oohing and aahing at how grand and large it was. It had enough rooms to house a large family.

Aidan stood by and watched with a smile. He loved to see the excited child in me.

"Okay, girls, this is where I leave you." He came toward me. I fell into his strong arms. "I've got a heavy schedule of meetings, angel. Have fun. I'll call you when I'm done. Okay?" His eyes glowed with a warm, gentle smile. "Now, don't get into trouble." He waved his finger at me with a mock authoritative expression.

Tabitha said, "I'll make sure that she doesn't."

CHAPTER SIXTEEN

———◆◇◆———

WE DECIDED TO GO to lunch first. Although Mike had offered to drive us around, we decided to walk in order to soak up the ambiance of the bustling avenue.

An appetizing aroma of garlic, hot dogs, and burgers floated through the air, making me hungry. We'd lunched on the plane, but I'd only managed a few bites of a sandwich after nerves robbed my appetite.

As we moved along, I noticed the black Mercedes following us. I supposed Aidan had requested Mike keep an eye on us. I didn't mind. After what had happened back at the estate, having someone watching over us, offered comfort.

Nevertheless, I made sure that I didn't pack the drama in with my mental baggage. Determined not to allow it to accompany me to New York, I'd pushed it away decisively.

Just as we were about to pass the Dolce and Gabbana emporium, Tabitha stopped. "Can we go in there, please?"

"I'm starving, Tabs. Let's grab something, then we'll go in. What do you think?"

She nodded. "Okay."

We looked about for somewhere. It didn't take long before we came across an attractive intimate café.

"How's this?" Tabitha pointed.

I peered through the window and was instantly drawn to the establishment's moody appeal via the black-and-white photos, memorabilia, and artifacts. "I like it. Let's go in there."

The menu was Italian, which suited me. I was in the mood for carbs, so I ordered spaghetti Bolognese and salad. Tabitha, who'd eaten a full lunch on the plane, opted for coffee and cake.

As we sat at the window table, watching the grand parade go by in their varied shades of fashion, a couple of men approached our table.

Dressed in stylish suits, they looked to be in their mid-thirties. Tabitha was all smiles and accommodating, which occasioned a kick from me under the table. I didn't feel like the company of strangers.

Meanwhile, oblivious to my subtle entreaties, Tabitha smiled sweetly at their banter, while I sighed silently with frustration. Considering Tabitha's insatiable appetite for attention, it was only predictable that we would attract the attention of stray men.

"Right, you're from LA, then?" asked the tall, blond, handsome stranger.

Having placed a forkful of spaghetti into my mouth, I had to swallow it and wipe my mouth before answering. "Yes. We're just here for a couple of days. My fiancée has some meetings to attend." I made sure I emphasized the fiancée bit and even flashed the impressive jewel beaming off my finger.

His face lit up with appreciation when he noticed the large diamond. Since we were in the ritzier part of New York, I suspected that they were accustomed to unabashed displays of wealth in the shape of big dazzling rocks.

The tall, dark, and handsome one was clearly taken with Tabitha. His eyes moved from her beautiful rosy-cheeked face to her cleavage and back again.

"Are you here with your fiancée, too?" he asked.

A sweet little curl formed on her lips as she shook her head.

"Do you mind if we join you for a drink?"

Shit. We'd been in New York for one minute, and the invites had already started.

Without consulting me, Tabitha nodded.

I jumped in quickly. "We've got a tight schedule, I'm afraid." A subtle narrowing of my eyes cast a "what the fuck?" at Tabitha.

"What about later on?" the dark-haired man asked. I could see he was dying to get with Tabitha. While his friend, whose eyes had not left my breasts, remained quiet.

Determined not to give him anything, I remained deadpan—no pretty-girl smile or breathy responses, like my cock-teasing friend was doing.

Tabitha gazed at me and bit her lip. She wanted to. I could see it.

I answered for her. "Might be difficult. Her fiancée's joining us for dinner."

Now it was my turn to get kicked under the table.

When they got the message and left, Tabitha said, "Now, why did you go and do that?"

"What do you mean? It was blatantly obvious he wanted you. He wasn't going to catch up and talk about the weather, was he?"

She laughed. "He was sexy, though."

"Tabs, need I remind you that you're engaged to be married and that your future husband's son is here with us?"

"Yeah, I know. But a little pre-marital fling wouldn't hurt."

"Fuck, Tabs. You're a restless little minx."

"I know." She cast her eyes down at her hands, then she looked up at me with a big smile. "And loving it."

I could do little but laugh. She was ridiculously changeable.

She stood up. All was forgotten, and Tabitha was back into party mode. "Are we ready for showtime?"

"Where to first?" I asked.

"Where do you think?" she asked with her hands on her hips.

"Um... let me guess. Does it start with a D?"

"Yeah, you bet. Let's go a go-go," she said, back her childish self. She'd forgotten all about Mr. Knight-In-Shining-Armani.

When we were greeted in Italian by a bevy of shop assistants as excitable as young children, it seemed as if we'd stepped into a nightclub. The only things missing were pulsing lights. The music was there, however, pumping away loudly while the staff danced about the customers.

"Do you think they're on cocaine?" whispered Tabitha, dragging me by the hand straight to a rack of jeans.

A young man approached me, and with a heavily accented, feminine voice, exclaimed, "Oh... but this little dress is beautiful."

Another shop assistant joined in with his crooning approval of my Mondrian-inspired mini.

"Thanks. It belonged to my mother," I said.

"Oh, it's an original. I love it." He touched the fabric. "I'm crazy about the sixties."

"Thanks. I'm rather fond of it myself. My mother bought it on Carnaby Street," I said.

"In London?" His eyes lit up as he kissed his fingers. I could have told him I was about to give him a lump of gold, such was his pleasure. "*Signorina*, it really suits you."

"Thanks. Excuse me for a minute." I smiled and headed over to Tabitha, who held up a pair of jeans that were ripped and worn out.

"You're quite a hit in this little town with that dress of yours," said Tabitha.

"Yeah, it's a pleasant departure from being poked fun at," I said.

"But you persist anyway," said Tabitha.

"Well, why shouldn't I?"

"True. You're one of a kind, Clarissa Moone. So, what do you think?" She held up two pairs of jeans, both equally worn.

"They're ripped and pretentious."

"It's called distressed, I believe," she said, laughing at my sardonic scowl.

I snorted.

She studied the price tag and scrunched her face. "The price tag's distressing. That's for sure."

I giggled at her dry tone. "If you want them, Tabs, I'll buy them. Aidan told me to go hard."

A cheeky glint coated her eyes. "Did he just?"

"Oh, Tabs, you've got a one-track mind."

"Well, when you use the word hard and Aidan in one sentence, what do you expect?"

"True." I smiled and felt a warm glow in my cheeks, recalling Aidan going deliciously hard on me just that morning. "Anyway, if you want them, they're yours."

She hugged me and squealed with delight.

The same sales assistant that had spoken to me sashayed over. "Can I help?"

Tabitha held up two pairs of jeans. "Can I try these on?"

"But of course." He held his chin. "Mm... you may need one size smaller."

"Oh? Do you think? I'm normally this size," she said.

"These are Italian sizes," he replied, handing her two pairs of jeans. "Depends if you want them to fit you very well." He raised a brow. And we giggled. He looked as if he plucked his eyebrows, and in a loose silk polka-dot shirt and super-tight red pants, he embodied the look-at-me style characteristic of that brand.

"Go and try them on. I'm just going over there to the dresses," I said.

"I'm Giancarlo," he said, holding out his soft, well-manicured hand. I shook it. "I'm Clarissa."

He leaned in close. "Clarissa, can I ask you a favor?"

"Sure," I said.

"Can I take a photo of you for our board?"

That was so unexpected, my mouth opened with a stretched "Oh?"

He smiled at my shocked expression. "We do that from time to time with some of our customers. The more expressively dressed ones. And this little dress is one I want to capture."

"Why not?" I touched my braids and swept a stray strand away from my face.

"Just as you are, Clarissa. *Sei una donna bellissima.*"

"Thank you," I said. The little I knew of Italian suggested that he was complimenting me.

"Massimo, *viene qui.*" He gesticulated to his colleague, who was just as feminine, with a sway to his hips.

"*Un foto, per favore,*" he said.

The young man took out his phone and framed it before us. Giancarlo put his arm around me, and I smiled.

"*Perfetto,*" Massimo sang.

He studied the shots and kissed his fingers. The scene was like something out of an Italian movie. It seemed surreal as the two effusive Italians spoke over each other.

"Ah...*que bella,*" he said. He showed me the shots. They were fun, to be sure.

"Do you want me to send it to you?" he asked.

I shrugged. "No, it's okay."

"Facebook?"

"I'm afraid I don't really use it," I said.

His head pushed back. "A beautiful girl like you. So stylish and about town, I am surprised." His eyes went to my finger and noticed my gleaming diamond. "Oh, a rich fiancée?"

I nodded and smiled. "Can you show me some dresses now, if that's okay?"

"*Ma si, signorina, subito.*" He crooked his finger and wiggled along. "*Viene.*"

Tabitha called out. I looked at him. "I need to go to my friend."

He tagged along like a sweet little puppy. Although he'd jumped right into our private space, I liked him. He had a sweet smile, and he did seem genuinely amiable, and not in a sickly need-to-make-a-sale way.

Tabitha stepped out in her ripped jeans. They fitted her like a glove.

"They look fantastic, Tabs."

Giancarlo nodded in agreement. "Very nice."

She turned to study her bottom. "They don't make my butt look too big?"

"No way. If anything, they're very flattering. And the little rips below the butt are very sexy."

"Aren't they?" Her big green eyes shone. "I love them. And they're so damn comfortable."

"They don't look it. They're stuck to your skin," I said.

"They're stretch," said Giancarlo. "What did I tell you? I bet they're the ones I suggested to you?"

She nodded. "They're really pricey, Clary."

"Nonsense. Let's take them. I'm just going to check the dresses. If there's anything else you want, grab it."

Tabitha hugged me. "You're the best."

When I saw the rack of silk florals, I let out a long sigh.

Giancarlo smiled. "Beautiful, yes. They've just come in. The colors are magical."

I stroked one of the silk dresses. "This one, I love."

His eyes narrowed as he studied my body before taking one off the rack. "This is your size, I believe. Would you like to try it?" He pointed to the dressing room.

I stood before the mirror. It fitted me as if it had been cut for my body. The bodice was low enough to show a sexy décolletage, my breasts pouting just enough to be feminine but not in a sleazy way. If anything, the crossover design supported and lifted my breasts. It was helped by ruching under the bust and around the waist, followed by a straight-lined skirt. The dress was delightfully 1950s. And the colors were truly magical—pinks that bled into burgundy, mauve, and purple against a creamy satin background left me purring like a kitten.

Tabitha said, "Oh my God, Clary, that's so gorgeous."

I was all smiles.

Giancarlo raced over and slapped his cheek. "*Bellisima.* You look like Loren or one of those beautiful, glamorous actresses from classic Hollywood with that figure. *Signorina... mama mia.*"

Both Tabitha and I looked at each other and smiled at his theatrics.

"I agree," said someone with a deep male voice behind me.

I turned, and an older man in a three-piece suit stood there. He was distinguished, with flecks of gray in his dark hair. He ate me alive with his sparkling blue eyes. His confident lingering stare seemed to say, "I'd like to make love to you slowly and deeply."

When Tabitha knocked me in the ribs, I admonished her with a sharp side-glance.

"That dress had you in mind when it was designed," he said.

"Thank you," I said, smiling shyly. He was making my face heat up. His eyes had that bedroom glow about them, for certain.

"Are you from around here?" he asked.

"No. I'm from LA. Just visiting," I said.

"How about a drink?" he asked. Mm... he was indeed confident.

I shook my head. "I can't, really. I'm here with my fiancée."

He stared down at my finger. "Oh, I see. Nice rock. He's one hell of a lucky guy."

"Daddy, can I have this?" asked a teenage girl holding up a jacket.

"Anything you like, darling." He returned his focus to me. "It's her birthday."

I nodded. I was feeling cold, and my nipples were showing. He noticed, of course. His eyes darkened, and I crossed my arms.

He smiled. "I hope you enjoy your stay here. It's a spectacular dress for an equally spectacular woman." He cast me another lingering gaze and handed me his card. "Here, just in case you want to see a few sights." His lips curved up suggestively before he left to join his daughter.

"Whoa. What was that about?" asked Tabitha, following me back into the dressing room. "One could have cut the air with a knife. The sexual tension was electric. Was he sex on legs, or what?"

I laughed. "You and older men."

"But, come on, Clary, you did like him a little. I saw your little goosebumps. His eyes fucked you, well and truly."

"Tabs, need I remind you that I'm madly in love with Aidan?"

"But you're still allowed to look. And he wore that suit oh so well."

"I think I need to buy this dress."

"You so do, sister. It's a knockout." Tabitha stared at the price and whistled. "Shit. That's one big price tag."

It read ten thousand dollars. "Hmm... isn't it? Do you think it's too extravagant? I mean, I do love it."

"You must. And Aidan did tell you to go hard," she said, waggling her eyebrows.

I giggled. We made our way to the register and passed a rack of T-shirts with DG on them.

Tabitha stopped to stare at them.

"Get one if you like. It would look cute with the jeans," I said.

Tabitha selected one with a diamante insignia. "How's this?"

I nodded. I was not a T-shirt girl—only when lounging around privately. But they did suit Tabitha, and turquoise was a pretty color.

After paying, we said our goodbyes. It was with great fanfare, double kisses on cheeks and all. As we were about to step onto the pavement, Giancarlo ran up to us and handed me a few passes. "If you're looking to go out clubbing, this is my friend's club. It's all the rage. Here are a few passes for you."

I took them. "Thanks, that's so kind of you."

He smiled and we left.

"Clubbing. Yay! Clary, let's. Do you think it's a gay club?" Tabitha asked, skipping along.

I shrugged. "I'll see what Aidan wants to do first. I'm not sure if I'm in the mood for techno music. It's not my thing."

"You're so last century, Clary." She linked her arm with mine, and we sprang along the pavement, weaving in and out of the crowd.

When we arrived at Tiffany's, I stopped. "I *must* go in there, Tabs."

I wanted to buy Aidan a wedding ring and have it engraved. I stood at the counter. The sales assistant's eyes opened wide when noticing my diamond ring. It had become a predictable reaction from all of those who saw it.

"I'd like to see your male wedding bands."

"Yes, madam. Do you know his size?"

I bit my bottom lip. "No. I suppose that's silly of me. But can I have a look and see what you have that's a little different?"

"Different? By that, you mean not plain like the traditional band. Stones?"

"Yeah, maybe." I thought about this for a moment. "Have you got anything with sapphires?" Aidan's sparkling blue eyes entered my mind.

He went off, then brought back some rings with large sapphires. They were all ostentatious, and I didn't think Aidan would go for them.

My eyes landed on one with a sapphire amongst elaborate Celtic scroll. I imagined it sitting regally on Aidan's large hand.

"That's very nice," said Tabitha. "And it's masculine. It's a gorgeous color."

The old jeweler nodded. "Yes, it's a quality sapphire. One of the best cuts available set against a platinum band. Top range," he said, looking at me.

"I want it," I said. "We can always adjust it if need be."

"Of course, madam. However, it's not a traditional band."

"True. Can you show me some bands, as well? Are there any that are engraved with scrolls?"

He shuffled off. He was so old that I imagined he'd been there for half a century.

When he returned, Tabitha, who had obviously had the same thought, asked, "Were you here in the sixties? Did you meet Holly Golightly?"

"Tabs, don't ask the poor man silly questions."

His baggy, spectacled eyes peered up at me. "Dear girl, if I had a dollar for each customer that asked me that question, I'd be a rich man. We have tours of women who come in and want to get rings engraved, only to never pick them up."

I shook my head in disbelief. "I'm a *Breakfast At Tiffany's* fan too. But I'll probably want to pick up this ring once it's engraved."

He nodded thoughtfully. "That, madam, I can understand." He went off and returned with a case of engraved platinum wedding bands.

I noticed one with swirling patterns and was immediately taken with it. "I love that one."

"Yes, its hand-engraved, a beautiful piece."

"What do you think, Tabs?"

She nodded. "Hmm... it's different and very ornate."

"It's a classical piece. For a man who likes beautiful things," he said, casting me a sweet smile.

"He does have a taste for classic designs." I held it up and fell in love with it. I only hoped that Aidan would. "I'll take both. Can I have them engraved and ready for the day after tomorrow? We'll be leaving then."

The jeweler's face shone with enthusiasm. 'Of course." He handed me a pad and pen. "Please write down what you wish engraved."

I looked at Tabitha. "What should I write?"

She shrugged.

I scribbled, "Aidan, my heart, body, and soul are eternally yours, love Clarissa."

Tabitha nodded. "That should do it."

"Is this too long?"

"No, we will make the heart a symbol if that works for you, and the love can also be a heart."

"Yes, perfect. Thank you so much." As I pulled out my credit card, I noticed a pair of ruby pendant earrings. "Can I have a look at those?" He dangled the pretty pieces in front of me. "They're gorgeous," I purred.

"They're so you, Clary."

"I'll take those as well. Thank you."

CHAPTER SEVENTEEN

We returned carrying a handful of bags filled with goodies. I was exhausted, and when the elevator arrived at the apartment, I fell into the Chesterfield armchair, and Tabitha sank onto a velvet sofa.

Aidan was still in his office because I could hear voices murmuring.

The voices grew louder, then the door opened. Out stepped Aidan, and when he saw me his face brightened. "You look like you've had a good workout."

"That I have, so has the credit card." My eyes brushed over his colleague. A tall, dark man appearing sharp in a well-tailored three-piece suit, which seemed to be the Fifth Avenue look. I personally preferred Aidan's loose linen shirt and chinos. Still, I sensed Tabitha's frame growing out of her earlier tired slouch.

"This is my fiancée, Clarissa, and her friend, Tabitha," said Aidan, turning to me. "This is Brad, my attorney."

Brad nodded in my direction. "Pleased to meet you. I've heard much about you." His attention then moved to Tabitha, and as he uttered the "pleased to meet you," his eyes remained on her.

"I thought we might catch up with Brad for dinner tonight. How's Italian sound?"

Tabitha looked at me. "Clarissa had spaghetti for lunch."

"I don't mind. I can eat Italian again," I said.

Aidan looked at me. "We can go somewhere else if you like."

"No. Honestly, I love pasta. You know that."

"I sure do. And at Carbone's, it's something else. Homemade pasta that melts in the mouth."

Brad nodded in agreement.

I smiled. "Then it's settled. We'll go there."

When we were alone in our room, I said, "Aidan, I hope you can forgive Tabitha and her flirty ways."

"To each their own, Clarissa. I respect she's your best buddy. For that only, and not because I enjoy her company. Although I do like seeing you both together, being all silly and girlish. I find that entertaining."

"You do?"

He undid my hair braid and ran his fingers through it to untangle it. "I do. Just as I love seeing your lush mane go all crinkly, and these sexy legs in that crazy little dress." He ran his hands up my thighs, and I melted.

My lips curled into a smile. It was hard to have a serious conversation around Aidan looking delectable in a shirt that was unbuttoned enough to show me the fine sprinkling of hair over his shapely chest. My addicted fingers could do little but sneak in. His very kissable lips curved up at one side, and his eyes lowered seductively.

But I couldn't get Tabitha and her man-eating ways out of my mind. "I'm just worried that after a few drinks, Tabitha may give Brad the wrong impression."

He took my hand and placed it back where it had been on his warm, firm chest. I could feel his heart vibrating against my palm. "Grant's no angel."

Once again, I removed my hand. "What do you mean?"

"Let's put it this way. If a chick tosses her panties at him at one of his gigs, he'll be sure to keep them and look for the owner."

"Are you telling me that he's likely to cheat on Tabitha?"

"Probably." Aidan's response was so cool and unaffected, my jaw dropped.

"But how can you be so accepting of that?"

"Clarissa, there's little I can do to change him. And Tabitha strikes me as the same, so they're really well suited, aren't they?"

"But Tabitha can be sensitive too, you know."

"As my father can be. They're adults, baby. What they choose to do in their private time is their business."

An uncomfortable knot had formed in my solar plexus. "What would you say if I acted like Tabitha?"

His lips tightened and his eyes had gone dark and intense. "I'd break the jerk's neck."

"And how do you think I'd feel if a woman tried to come on strong to you?"

"I'd expect you to do the same." His lips twitched. "Not break her neck, but perhaps pull her hair, something a bit more feminine. Or poison her. At least, I hope you would."

Unable to roll with his drollery, I said, "I would do more than pull her hair, Aidan. It would send me crazy with jealousy. Look at what happened with Jessica."

He finished undoing my hair and ran his fingers through it. As he massaged my scalp, I dissolved into the leather sofa.

"Clarissa, I am nothing like my father. Even in my crazy, fucked-up days. I never, I repeat, *never* cheated on Jessica. I'm a one-woman man. And to be honest, no woman has ever made me feel and come the way you do. I'm constantly hot around you, Clarissa." He undid the zipper to my dress, and his hands traveled to my breasts. His caresses sent shivers of excitement through me.

"You're the prize, Clarissa. Even the most seasoned player would happily become monogamous if it meant having you."

I smiled. "That's reassuring, Aidan, because I don't want anybody but you." I hooked my fingers inside his waistband and drew him close to me. My hand ran up and down his bulge.

His eyelids lowered as he sat by my side on the sofa. Opening my thighs, he hooked his finger inside my panties and ripped them off. That little destructive act always sent a lightning bolt through me.

"I feel like a pre-dinner snack," he said, running his tongue up my thigh.

Phew. Would it ever stop burning so deliciously? Somehow, I didn't think it possible. Just the mere smell of Aidan as I buried my face in his warm neck had me sighing. That distinct masculine scent oozing out of his skin exuded a powerful aphrodisiac. I breathed him in as I would a rose. It was a drug. My eyelids lowered as an intense ache overtook me. When his tongue tickled my engorged bud, I winced, and my body liquified.

I unzipped his pants and reached in for his pulsating erection.

An aroused sigh left his parted lips. "You're mine, baby, as is this little, wet, pussy."

· · · ● · ● · ● · ·

CROSSING MY ARMS, I hid my nakedness as I ran to the shower. Aidan chased me. He played some silly boogeyman and made stupid monstrous sounds. It was child's play. I loved every glorious minute of it.

Aidan laughed more and more each day. The intensity that he used to revert to when left to his own thoughts had vanished. After everything we'd been through, I sensed his relief. Two enemies no longer cast their vengeful shadows over our perfect lives.

In Bryce's case, it was more complex, because Aidan was saddened by his former buddy's descent into crime. If it weren't for the threat Bryce had posed for me, I think Aidan would've cried at Bryce's funeral. The fact that he even attended surprised me.

It added to my love for Aidan because it took a big heart to feel compassion for a man as selfish and warped as Bryce.

I still recalled Aidan's response when I questioned him over his decision to attend the funeral. "Princess, who are we to judge the fallen? There are often so many dark forces behind a person's descent into crime—a past riddled with abuse; violent and persistent bullying at school; or unaffectionate parents. Love makes us. It civilizes us. I don't think Bryce ever had that." His lips twitched as his natural stoicism fought off a lone tear.

Instead, I cried for him. More because of the sadness I felt for those who were alone and lost.

As we held each other tight, I thanked my late mother. Before Aidan came into my life, I never believed in the supernatural. But as I inhaled my lover's very essence, I was convinced that my late mother's spirit had delivered Aidan into my arms.

· · · ● · ● · ● · ·

TABITHA WAS IN A thick bathrobe with her hair in a towel when I entered. "I can't decide what to wear. What are you wearing?" she asked.

"The purple dress I picked up from the Vintage Bazaar."

"You're going all Goth. I suppose it will go with the ruby earrings you bought."

"That's what I thought." I walked to the window and stared out onto the busy street. There was so much to see and take in. It was an endless stream of life. But as my eyes stretched above their heads, a priceless view of the lush, green park made me pause for a breath.

Tabitha held up her prized jeans.

"They're a little too casual, Tabs."

She nodded.

"What about the red silk wrap-around dress we bought today?"

Her eyes sparkled with delight. "It's so sexy. Do you think? I could wear it with these ankle boots."

"Hmm... it would grunge it up a bit, I suppose. I like it."

"Yay!" Tabitha swung me around. "This is so much fun. Thanks for bringing me along, Clary." She went serious. "Is Aidan okay about all the things you bought me? Shit. You spent a fortune."

"I haven't actually had a chance to mention it," I said with a hint of a smile.

"Ah, I thought I could hear a bit of groaning and moaning. I figured it wasn't due to a tooth being pulled. Something a little more delicious being pulled?" Her eyebrows bounced up and down.

I laughed raucously. "You're wicked, Tabs. And I didn't realize the walls were so thin."

"Don't worry, sweetie. I owe you big time for all those wall-vibrating sessions back in our little place downtown."

"You sure do." I giggled. "There were times when I couldn't work out whether you were being strangled or whether you were actually enjoying it."

"Both," she said with a cheeky glint in her eyes.

"What?" I grimaced.

She laughed. "Just pulling your little leg. God, you're so gullible."

"Well, I don't know with you, Tabs. Especially with this whipping fetish you've suddenly developed."

She stripped out of her robe and stood in her lacy white bra and panties.

I thought of her earlier flirtation with Aidan's attorney. "Hmm...you look like you're getting ready for your own moany-groany session."

"Ha..." She giggled. "Yeah, Brad's pretty cute."

"What about Grant?"

"You keep asking me that. Look, Clarissa, there's something I need to tell you."

I hissed behind my teeth. "Should I sit down?"

"If you're going to bring your 1950's grandma attitude, then yes, do sit."

I rolled my eyes. "I'm not that old-fashioned. You're just wild."

"Mm... I suppose I am." She smirked. "Anyway, look, Grant and I have decided to swing."

"You mean swap partners?"

"All of that, and more."

"And more?"

She laughed at my scrunched look of disbelief. "We discussed it. As long as we use condoms, he's cool with it. And there's more to it, I suppose."

"What do you mean?"

Tabitha had that look she got when about to reveal something shocking—narrowing eyes, a reddening of her cheeks, and a twitchy little grin.

"He admitted one night while we were watching pornos that he'd like to watch me being fucked by another guy."

My mouth opened wide. "What? Porn? You watch those together?" At that moment, I really did sound like a 1950's grandma. I also realized just how straight my sex life with Aidan was. It was perfect, though. There were plenty of raunchy happenings between us, and I would have hated to rely on pornography to keep us aroused.

Before she could respond, I asked, "What happened to the jealous, 'I would cut his balls off' attitude you had, and not to mention Grant who, you told me was seriously jealous also?"

She shrugged. "We've changed. We're comfortable in our relationship, I suppose. He would do everything to protect me and knock someone out if they tried to take me away, and I guess I would be seriously pissed if Grant left me to marry someone else." She tied her wrap dress and looked in the mirror. "We're in love, Clary."

"It's a strange form of love. But who am I to judge? But I do worry about you. Are you ever going to stop being so restless?"

Tabitha turned and faced me. For the first time since arriving, I noted a shadow fall over her face. "I don't know. Life's short. Look at what happened with my family. All dead by the time they were forty. If I'm going to die young, at least I would've had a ton of fun."

"But you don't know for sure. I mean, your mom and dad were both heavy smokers. You don't smoke. You're as healthy as anything. And goodness knows you get plenty of exercise." I arched a brow.

Her face brightened. "Yeah, of the fun kind. None of that pounding on concrete for us girls."

"That's better." I studied her for a moment. "But still, that's so weird about you and Grant. I couldn't do it."

"I know that." She pulled at my hair playfully. "I just needed to let you know that if I decide to fuck Brad, then I have Grant's blessing."

I shook my head in disbelief. "Shit."

I recalled Aidan's blasé response earlier regarding Tabitha's predilection for flirting and just sighed with acceptance. "As long as you don't do it here. I couldn't stand that. I still find this difficult to deal with. You seemed so into each other."

"Grant and I are really in love. It's just that he's as sexually restless as I am. We discussed it and decided that it would be okay to have spontaneous experiences. Have you heard of polyamory?"

"Multiple partners?" I asked.

She nodded. "That's us. We even went to a meeting about it."

"And you're only telling me now?"

"There's been a lot happening in your world lately, Clarissa."

I nodded wistfully. "Yeah, true."

Although what Tabitha had just admitted wasn't easy for me to digest, I dropped out of my judgmental state and said, "Okay, better get ready, then. The purple Goth dress it is. Can you do my hair?"

She came over and hugged me. "I sure can. And thanks." She pulled away and smiled sadly.

I shrugged. "That's okay. Aidan's loaded. He doesn't mind."

"No, not that, though, yeah, thanks for that too, but thanks for understanding and accepting me for who I am."

"We're sisters." I hugged Tabitha. "I won't forget how you were always there, belittling my bullies with your smart tongue, and how you supported me all those months by paying rent and buying food for us. And never complaining about it. You used up all your inheritance on keeping us going."

"I'd do it again and again."

I left Tabitha choked up, even if this new polyamory direction of hers had left a strange taste in my mouth.

CHAPTER EIGHTEEN

TABITHA PUT MY HAIR up in a messy bun. It suited my purple silk-chiffon baby doll dress with tiered layers that flared out like a ballerina's costume and floated in the air when I spun around. The sleeves were transparent, with a delightful flounce at the wrist. As I stood before the mirror, I could see that Tabitha was right—it was very Morticia. Around my neck, I tied a thin velvet ribbon. The ruby pendant earrings finished off my outfit perfectly.

Aware that the night would be cool, I had splashed out and bought a black cashmere coat with a fur collar. I purred with delight when I saw the beautifully tailored knee-length coat, which happened to fit me like a glove. Even though the price tag was in the thousands, I had to have it.

Aidan looked deliciously handsome, as always, in cream trousers that fell with elegant perfection from his waist. A white silk shirt and sky-blue linen blazer hugged his large shoulders. I wanted to devour him. His hair pomaded back showed off his beautiful face—that nose with a slight bump, which only added to his male beauty. It was hard to breathe properly around him.

His eyes lit up. "Oh my, you sexy little goddess. I love that dress."

I spun around. "I feel like a dancer in it."

He drew a circle with his finger. "Again, but this time faster."

I pirouetted over and over again, giggling as I gave in to the dizzy delight of showing off my pretty dress and all that was below.

He ran his hand up my legs. "Mm... you look sensational, Clarissa."

"I'm not too Gothic."

"Splendidly so. I love all these looks, baby. I'm so glad you're not a blue-jeans-and-stretchy T-shirt girl."

"I do wear them sometimes."

He squeezed my butt. "Yes, I know, and I love you in them, especially without a bra. But I also love you being classy and unique when we're out. That's what I mean."

I stroked his jacket. "And I love this color on you, Aidan. The women of New York are going to be a little dewy tonight, staring at you."

He laughed. "Dewy?"

"I spent a truckload of money today." I grimaced.

"Good. The more, the better."

I shook my head in disbelief.

"Clarissa, it's only money."

"I know that, but there are many out there that could survive for a few months at the cost of this dress alone."

He raised a brow. "It's a sublime dress. I get your point, but beauty is worth everything. And you are that, my love."

"I also spent a fair bit on Tabitha."

"Good."

"Why are you so generous?"

He shook his head and shrugged. "Come on. Put on that pretty coat, and let's go. We're running late."

I slipped on my new cashmere coat and stood before the mirror. I'd opted for lace-up ankle boots. I loved the look. I turned and faced Aidan.

He shook his head. "You ought to be on the cover of Vogue. You look good enough to eat."

I leaned in and kissed his neck. A subtle whiff of cologne assaulted my senses. The deeper I drew, the more his male scent tantalized my senses. Drugged on Aidan, I took his arm and floated into the night.

If there were one thing one should do before leaving this earthly home, it was to taste homemade pasta. After I bit into the ravioli, mouth-watering flavors were unleashed onto my tongue. It was the sexiest meal I'd ever eaten, and so delicious I melted into my seat.

Always in tune with my moods, Aidan gazed at me, delighting in my fondness for food.

While Tabitha and Brad were lost in their own little world of seduction, I had Aidan's undivided attention as I explained to him the virtues of the Met Museum.

"I can't believe I'm going to see it, at last, Aidan. And that it is virtually across the road from us."

He wiped his lips and took a sip of red wine. "That's why I bought the apartment."

"I love it. I love New York. It's bubbling away with culture."

"Just wait until I take you to Paris, baby. That will make those delectable, rosy lips open wide."

"I can't wait for that. But for now, I have the Met tomorrow."

"I'd love to come along. I've been there often alone, but I'd like to share it with you. I particularly like the Egyptian antiquities."

"That's right. It's not just the paintings, but also artifacts. It's such a rich collection. I'm dying to see the Picasso's."

Aidan took a sip of wine. "It's probably not as comprehensive as Barcelona."

"I know, but still," I said. "There are some of his pre-Cubist works—his Toulouse Lautrec-inspired paintings. Did you know Picasso said, 'A great artist doesn't borrow he steals?'"

"That's one big confession coming from someone who launched the modernist movement."

I nodded. "He was the bridge between the classical era and the modern era, to be sure. Although Van Gogh and Cezanne got there first. They broke new ground, as did Turner for the Impressionist movement. In many ways, most art is copied. I see it as a form of curating—selecting images and ideas and mixing them to make something original."

Aidan nodded with an appreciative smile. "I love Turner. He's everything for me. I saw his works at the Tate. The seascapes are phenomenal. I fell into them. You know, I just sat and stared at them. The cry of the wind and the wild sea."

My skin rippled with love. "Are you real?" I asked.

His lips turned up at one end. "That's a question I often ask about you, angel." Alone in our own universe, our eyes locked, as Aidan took my hand and kissed it.

Leaving me to swoon, Aidan turned to Brad. "What time's the meeting in the morning?"

Brad's dark eyes had that glow of desire etched into them. Tabitha had drawn the lawyer into her web of seduction. I'd seen that look over and over again. An hour with Tabitha and men turned to putty. "Ah... ten a.m."

"How long?"

"Two hours at the most, I'd say."

Aidan looked at me. "Then we'll go together."

Excitement charged through me. "I'd love that."

Tabitha looked at me. "Let me guess. The Met?"

I nodded.

Turning to Brad, Tabitha said, "Clarissa has done nothing but talk about it all day. She's an art tragic."

Brad laughed. "As is Aidan."

Aidan reached over and took my hand again. It was like a badge of honor for both us, this little passion of ours.

The night was crisp. I was really cozy in my coat, while Tabitha, dressed in a thin cardigan, crossed her arms, and her teeth chattered. Brad took off his jacket and placed it over her shoulders. Her face lit up immediately with delight as she clasped it tightly around her.

As Aidan stood close with his arm around my waist, I felt so happy and light. I loved standing in the night and being amongst the clutter of individuality gliding along.

"So where to now?" Aidan asked, looking at me.

Tabitha jumped in. "Clarissa's holding some free passes to a club."

Aidan looked at me. "Do you want to go?"

"Do you?" I asked, as indecisive as always.

He looked at Brad. "What do you think?"

"I'm into it." His eyes were all over Tabitha. After a couple of wines, he'd become looser and more open about his attraction to her.

Tabitha nodded with predictable enthusiasm. "You bet. I'd love to dance off all those carbs."

I looked at Aidan. "Then let's, just for a while. We can always leave if it gets too much."

Aidan leaned in and kissed me. "Anything for you, sexy girl."

Mike was there waiting for us. Standing by the black Mercedes, he held the doors open for us and we slid in.

As we arrived at our destination, I noticed the line outside the dance club was dishearteningly long.

"I don't know about this," said Aidan. "What do you think?"

I shrugged. "Let's see. Tabitha's really good at cutting in line."

Standing next to me, Tabitha nodded. "Leave it to me." That determined wouldn't-take-no-for-an-answer expression was written all over her face.

We were suddenly figures of fascination with the colorful collection of clubbers queuing up.

I handed the passes to Tabitha, and she headed to chat with the doormen. They glanced over at us, returning a serious, sharp nod back to Tabitha.

"I think she's managed to swing it," I said to Aidan.

Tabitha gesticulated for us to come along, and without fuss, we were shuttled into the large pulsing room.

The walls were ablaze with big splotches of paint, with large Jackson Pollack-inspired paintings hung everywhere. In lit-up cages, scantily clad males, females, and non-gender danced with wild abandon. It felt as if I were in a movie. It was everything and more of what I'd expected.

"This is so cool!" yelled Tabitha.

The music was predictably deafening and ribcage thumping. We went upstairs to a dark corner and settled there. It wasn't as crowded as I had expected considering the large line of people who'd been waiting outside.

Aidan ordered bourbon for himself and champagne for Tabitha and me, while Brad opted for a beer.

Tabitha leaned in. "Let's dance."

I looked at Aidan.

"I'll sit this out, baby. Go and have fun. I look forward to watching you." He stroked my dress and smiled with his liquid blue eyes.

As I stood up, I heard a screechy cry from behind me. I turned and saw Giancarlo from the boutique.

"You came. And wow, I love this," he said, lifting the silk fabric of my dress. "You look spectacular, *Bambina.*"

"Thanks. This is my fiancée, Aidan, and this is Brad. Tabitha, you know."

He nodded to everyone, then returned his eyes to Aidan.

He whispered, "He's beautiful, your man."

I smiled.

"You are going to make beautiful *bambini*."

I smiled at his dark, expressive eyes twinkling playfully. "Come on. Let's dance."

He sashayed along, linking his arm with Tabitha's and mine.

All eyes were on us. We made a colorful trio. Giancarlo wore tight white pants and a bomber jacket emblazoned with a design of blue-and-white Moroccan tiles depicting a sun.

I loved feeling my dress floating as I spun around on the dance floor. Giancarlo moved his hips about wildly, while Tabitha showed off her feminine curves as her silk wrap splayed open, revealing her lace stockings.

Such was her alluring presence that a couple of guys came and joined us, dancing up really close. So close, I felt one of them breathing behind me.

Aidan was there in a shot as he moved through the swooning women who were swaying in his direction. Oblivious to the hormonal eruption he was causing, Aidan claimed me, and we danced close to each other. With those blue eyes smiling away, Aidan was a natural when it came to dancing.

Brad joined Tabitha and stood behind her, simulating a sex act. Or so it seemed. It was the way to dance. I noticed most on the dance floor were in the same sexy mood, with butts grinding against pelvises.

Mm... I couldn't wait to do that at home with my naked, well-endowed lover.

After one more tune, Aidan and I returned to our table. I left Giancarlo, who was hitting on a young man.

Aidan filled my glass. "You're driving every man crazy in here tonight, angel."

"And so are you. Both women and men. You look so handsome." I fell into his arms, and our lips met.

"Do you want to go soon?" he asked.

"I do," I said, thinking about the little strip show I would perform for him at home.

CHAPTER NINETEEN

◆◇◆

AIDAN

DESPITE THE FACT THAT I'd enjoyed myself in New York, it was great to be home. The highlight for me had been visiting the Met with Clarissa. It would have been the perfect weekend was it not for the Tabitha-and-Brad story. That left a bad taste.

Clarissa mentioned that Tabitha crept in during the early hours, suggesting she didn't go home with him. It still made me feel uneasy.

They say you get the partner you deserve, and in many ways, Tabitha was a good match for my equally wild father. Still, I'd hoped this match would be different. I thought of sweet Sara and how she'd suffered over the years due to my father's indiscretions. At least Tabitha was tougher than that.

Who was I to judge others? I kept telling myself.

Deep down inside, I was a conservative man where love was concerned. The possessive love I had for Clarissa overwhelmed me at times. She didn't seem to mind, however. I was grateful for that. Because as much as I tried to control my emotions, my knuckles always went white whenever men ate Clarissa with their eyes. Just like at the nightclub in New York. In that witchy purple dress, she was a knockout. No woman had Clarissa's grace and sexiness, in my eyes, at least. She was pure female, naturally blessed. The sway of her hips sent men crazy. Those big brown eyes on first glance appeared innocent and sweet, but then a little fire burned deep, especially whenever she looked down at my hard cock.

It was the same way I burned out of control when she opened her legs and showed me her pretty, wet pink pussy. No woman had ever affected me that way. And the fact that no man had ever been there made my heart explode. Knowing that she was all mine, that I was her first and would be her only lover, had made me religious. Because I was constantly thanking God for bringing Clarissa into my arms.

With his tail wagging and body wiggling with excitement, Rocket hobbled over to me.

I bent down. "Hey, buddy." Rocket's friendly dark eyes made me smile and lightened my mood. He always managed to elevate me in a way that no doctor or drug could. Clarissa was the only other person that had that magic twinkle in her eyes. Not that I could compare them. The love I had for my dog was undefinable. Especially after he saved our lives. Giving him bones and special treats just didn't quite meet the appreciation and gratitude I felt toward my loyal furry friend.

"Hello, Rocket," sang Clarissa, bending to pat him. He tried to jump up, but I could see it was a struggle. It broke my heart. He had always been such an athletic creature, leaping and taking off with lightning speed, hence his name. Nevertheless, I preferred him like that rather than dead. I wasn't ready to lose him yet. We'd been through a lot, my dog and I. Although he was still a little shaky on his hind leg where he'd been shot, he did seem himself again.

Rocket followed along after us. After Roland told me that the vet had checked him and that he was doing well, I decided to allow him up the stairs.

Will was on my mind. He'd called me while I was in New York, and I told him I'd catch up when we returned.

I left Clarissa to unpack and headed down to the kitchen.

Will stood in front of a large pot stirring when I entered. The aroma was as appetizing as always. He was a brilliant, sought-after chef who could have named his price in any establishment. He turned and flinched.

"Sorry. I didn't mean to startle you."

"Hey. How was the trip?" he asked.

"Yeah. Good, thanks." I shifted about. "Have you got a moment?"

"Sure." His focus went for the bottle of bourbon on the bench. He held up the bottle. "Do you want a drop?"

As it was late afternoon, I nodded. "Sure."

After he'd poured the drinks, we headed for the dining room and sat down. I looked up and noticed the gilded framed Mucha prints that Clarissa had brought home.

They looked glorious against the red walls. I felt lighter suddenly, which was a bonus because this was not an easy conversation.

"Look, Aidan, the whole Susana thing. I didn't know she was connected to that Howard prick." He'd taken off his chef's cap and rubbed his bald head.

I nodded. "Yeah, it took all of us by surprise. Linus included." I studied Will's face for signs. I wondered how he was toward our security guard, who I hadn't fired.

He exhaled a loud breath. "Linus. Yeah, she was fucking him, as well." He shook his head. "Fuck, I was so naïve. But you know how it is. Pretty blonde, tits hanging out, that ass that wiggled up close." He sighed again.

I sensed he missed her.

"She was attractive, I suppose," I said, not hiding my disinterest in her. "But she was a honeypot. A devious design to get to me."

"I'm sorry, man. I should've found out more. But she came at me, you know?"

"It was her way of staying here. I can see that now. Clarissa wanted her out. Greta didn't like her either. But because I knew you had formed an attachment, I let her stay. That was part of her scheme. Then she got to Linus so that she could lure him away from his post."

"I'm surprised you've let him stay."

"Yeah, well, he's an old buddy from the army. A good guy. You know that. You've known him for years."

He smiled grimly. "Sure do. We came to blows, you know? Not proud of it. I came off second best."

"Linus is a monster when it comes to battle. That's why I'm keeping him. He's a strong sonofabitch. He's deeply affected by this and hasn't stopped apologizing. Forgiveness is not easy for me, considering the danger he put Clarissa, Rocket, and me in. But I know a broken man when I see one."

"We've since made up. We had a night out on the town and talked it through," said Will.

"Good to hear. I'm relieved. You guys are family to me."

"I know, Aidan. That's why this has sat so fucking badly. So are you going to have that bitch charged?"

"You bet," I said. "Susana was an accessory to murder. I want her locked away. I'll never forget that scowl on her face. I could see by the contempt in her eyes that she was prepared to spend a lifetime devising ways to reap revenge."

"She was good. I'll give her that much," said Will. His eyes had a sad glint.

"I'm sure you'll meet another woman who'll at least be the real thing, Will."

He shook his head. "No. I'm not the marrying kind, Aidan. I like my life how it is. Whenever I need a woman, I know where to find them. LA is filled to the brim with Susana's. I prefer to pay for it with cash than with blood, though."

I stood up and patted Will on the arm. "Are the fish biting?"

His face brightened. "Yeah, this morning, we went out. We got a five pounder."

"Fantastic."

"For dinner?"

"You bet. Love my fish." I tapped my belly. "Have you been able to find a temporary maid until Greta gets back?"

"Not yet. I wanted to wait until you got back. I figured you would need some serious background checks first."

"I will. We can make do for the next day or so. I'll ask Clarissa to call an agency in the morning."

My steps lightened after I talked to Will.

It had been more awkward with Linus earlier. Shuffling his feet and looking downcast, he mumbled something about being forever indebted to me. I told him that although it was a serious slip-up, I'd forgiven him and patted him on the arm. His large black eyes glistened as he nodded in gratitude. It was sad to see such a big man fighting back tears. All I could do was reassure him, and to explain that I understood the male's weakness for a good blowjob. His large, fleshy lips curled up into a sad smile, and we left it at that.

All was how it should be. I looked forward to Greta returning, even though I was glad she hadn't experienced the drama. I did wonder how she'd take Grant's engagement to Tabitha. Greta didn't miss a thing, especially with my father being her twin. She read him well, despite their extremely different lifestyles. While my father had been out gigging every night, ending it with a groupie in his arms, Greta's cloistered existence revolved around me.

That was why I loved and respected Greta. The sacrifices she made, not even a mother would have gone that far. I even encouraged her to be like the others, but she'd always return a look that was both steadfast and reserved.

My father once told me that Greta had her heart broken when she was young and that it had taken her half a lifetime to heal. Still, Julian Moone was worth the wait. He was, after all, a perfect gentleman—handsome, sensitive, goodhearted, intelligent, and witty. I couldn't have been happier for Greta and me, knowing that he was to be my father-in-law.

My guitars sat waiting for me. I needed a session badly.

I'd left Clarissa with her head buried in the heavy catalog from the Met that we'd brought back. She was so absorbed in it that when I dropped in to see how she was, she gazed up from the book with those soft, beautiful eyes. Clarissa assured me she was happy doing her own thing until dinner. I leaned against the door, and a profound sense of satisfaction overtook me. With her hair down, no makeup, barefooted, legs stretched out, it was a nourishing image that my soul feasted on.

As I plugged in my prized red Gibson, the guitar I called Ferrari, I felt seriously blessed. I wasn't sure what lucky star was over me, or whether anything like that existed. But to have Clarissa home safe, while I held a seriously hot guitar, life just couldn't be better.

After dinner, we decided to watch Jerry Lewis's *The Nutty Professor*. We needed a good laugh, and I hadn't seen that film since I was young. It wasn't long, however, before I got distracted. As my hands crept under Clarissa's blouse, I felt the warmth of her naked breasts. I hit the pause button.

Clarissa's eyelids grew heavy and that pretty glow she got when aroused painted her dainty features. Apart from her breakfasting on my cock in the shower, as she did nearly every morning, we hadn't made love that day.

"Get naked, princess, and let me look at you." My cock pushed hard against my jeans. I unzipped them to release the ache.

Clarissa smiled and slipped off her T-shirt. My hands were hungry for her curves. I kissed her hot, warm lips, my tongue driving in deep as I lifted her, and carried her to bed.

CHAPTER TWENTY

───◆◇◆───

I WAS COMING BACK from a walk with Rocket when Chris came up on my phone. I picked up. "Hey, how's it going?"

"Yeah, man, not bad, I suppose."

I could tell he wasn't in a good state. "What's happened?"

"Look, um... can we talk?"

"Sure. I happen to be heading to Venice now," I said.

"I can meet you there if you like," he said.

"No. I'll come to your studio. I wouldn't mind checking out some of your latest work."

"Sure, if you want to do it that way. This isn't about making a sale, though, Aidan." He didn't sound like himself. Even with that lazy drawl, Chris's tone normally rang with devil-may-care positivity.

"I'll catch you in a couple of hours, Chris."

"Thanks, man."

There was something in his voice that spelled trouble. Was it money? The law? A junkie's life was one constant revolving door of mayhem. I would have told him to fuck off, but there was something about Chris that made it hard not to like him. Perhaps it was his ridiculous talent or that charming, languid honesty. One thing I did know—the vets loved his no-bullshit approach. The program, I believed, was a success due to him.

I found Clarissa in the yard drawing. What a sight. My heart always leaped whenever I saw her. It was an image I could never tire of. If anything, my need for her grew stronger and stronger.

Her hair was bunched up and her swanlike neck made my mouth salivate. Only that morning I'd drank her dry while her whispery sighs undid me. My cock thickened as I recalled spanking her peachy butt. Any excuse and I had her over my knees. Her girlish giggles transmitted straight to my cock.

She looked up and smiled.

"Hey, baby. Show me," I said.

Her lips drew a tight line. "I've only just started. It's nothing yet."

I leaned over her, my hands on her shoulders, massaging her.

On her pad was a drawing of the old willow.

"It's really good. You're improving all the time."

She sighed. "I'm practicing more than ever. Thanks to you and this amazing lifestyle."

I kneeled down and kissed her warm, cushiony lips. "After the wedding, do you want to go to Europe?"

Her eyes opened wide. "That would be sensational, Aidan. Only..."

I shook my head. "What?"

"I'm really scared of flying. You saw how I was on that recent trip to New York. I was a mess."

Nodding with sympathy, I replied, "The smaller planes are more jittery than the larger ones. We could fly commercial, first class."

She nodded slowly. "If you like. Although I've always had this ridiculous urge to go by ship. I know that sounds awfully old-fashioned.

"We'll go by ship then if you like."

Her mouth opened, and her eyes lit up with wonder. She looked so young and full of promise, my heart melted.

"Aidan, I've always dreamt of that, you know? I couldn't think of anything more divine than to cruise around Europe."

"We can take a liner to London. Once we're on the continent, we'll rent a large, comfortable cruiser."

"I can't wait." Her brow drew in. "But will you be okay with all that spare time on the ship? I mean, I've got my books and drawings."

I laughed. "I'm not as restless as all that. I've got you to keep me happy. One month, with my feet up reading books and magazines, and watching movies, sounds fantastic. I can't wait."

"What about your music?"

"I'll drag along my acoustic. That should keep me engrossed, as will you, baby, and all your little performances." I raised a brow. Clarissa had demonstrated great talent for stripping and exotic dancing.

"You won't get bored?"

I laughed. "Oh, Clarissa. I could make love to you day and night and still not get enough. You're beautiful. Every square inch of you is delicious. My eyes, tongue, mouth, and cock are totally addicted. Your expressive, tight pussy leaves me breathless."

She winced. "It does? How so?"

"I dug up a copy of the *Karma Sutra* from my library the other day. By the end of our trip, I expect we will have tried every position."

"But you didn't answer me, Aidan."

"You're velvety, creamy, super tight, and seriously responsive. My cock loves how you squeeze tightly around it when you're coming."

She fell into my arms. "You make me feel hot just talking about it."

"I have to go downtown. I'm dropping in on Chris. He asked to see me about something."

"Do you mind if I come? I need some watercolors, and I wouldn't mind seeing what Chris has been working on."

"Of course, you can, Angel."

Chris greeted us with his typical lazy smile. "Hey Aidan, Clarissa."

"I thought I'd tag along to see what you've been working on," said Clarissa.

"Yeah, sure. Come on in. I'm having a Pollack moment."

I laughed. "You make it sound like a disorder. Let me guess. You're splashing paint about?"

Chris chuckled. "Yeah, man. Sometimes I just need to let go."

Clarissa stopped. "Aidan, I left my bag in the car."

"Do you want me to get it?"

"No, I will," she insisted.

I nodded and stroked her rosy cheek. "Okay, sweetheart."

I followed Chris into his studio.

"This is a good time to tell you before Clarissa returns," said Chris. A grimace shadowed his face.

"What's that?" I asked.

"You know I've been knocking about with Jessica."

I nodded.

"I saw her last night. She was shit-faced and confided something that was so disturbing it kind of robbed me of sleep and has been hanging heavily over me since."

My eyes remained transfixed on him.

"She told me she hired a hitman to take Clarissa out."

Blood raced through my veins, and my knuckles stretched the flesh around my fist. "What? The car chase, you mean?"

"Yeah, that. She was seriously drunk. I let her have it and tossed her out. She banged on the door, threatening me." He laughed grimly. "She's fucking trouble, that one."

"Fuck" was the best I could say.

His sleep-deprived eyes glistened with sincerity. "I like you and Clarissa. You're good people. Most people look at me as a junkie, a drop-out. I've lost every job because of it. And you still gave me a chance."

My head was swimming in too many directions to take in Chris's words of sincerity. "Would you be prepared to testify?"

He nodded.

It suddenly dawned on me that Clarissa was not with us. Why was she taking so long?

"I better check on Clarissa. I'll be back in a minute."

When I stepped onto the street, there was the car but no Clarissa. I was still raging after Chris's revelation, and my blood pumped so hard through my veins that my heart felt like a hard rock banging desperately against my chest.

The dirty gray street was spinning around. It was an out-of-body experience. I couldn't breathe. I yelled out her name, which echoed back with desolation. My senses returned, and I called 911.

I looked about to see if there were cameras.

Chris came out.

"She's gone. Chris. Fuck."

Just as Chris uttered, "Jessica" my phone buzzed.

It was private. I picked up.

"Hello, Aidan." It was Jessica.

"What have you done with Clarissa?"

She laughed. "What makes you think I've got her?"

"Stop fucking playing games. What do you want?"

"I want you, Aidan."

"Where's Clarissa?" The phone was wet in my palm. Such was my anxiety, I squeezed the life out of it.

"She's safe. My men are salivating over her right now."

I yelled, "You fucking bitch, Jessica! If anything happens to her... if anyone touches a hair on her head..."

"Here's a picture for you."

A picture came through of Clarissa. Her blouse was half torn. My heart exploded into glass shards. A mixture of frustration and violent hatred gripped every sinew in my body.

As I held the phone, shaking, Chris called the police.

I pressed my beeper for James. He had a sophisticated tracking device linked to my phone. Within a moment, he would be capable of tracing the location of the caller.

"What the fuck do you want from me, Jessica?"

"I want us to meet. Then I will lay down my demands."

"You must promise me to keep Clarissa safe."

"Hmm... I've got two very horny security guards here that are taken with her. That's for sure. It's going to be hard to stop them from fucking her."

Blood boiled and drowned my mind of reason. "I will fucking kill you, Jessica if any of your men touch her."

"This is the deal. You come here and fuck me in front of your little girl, then I'll let her go. Then you'll be mine."

My breakfast raced up my esophagus. "Send me the details. I'm coming now."

"Not so fast, big boy. No heavies and no cops. We'll do it this way. I'll meet you at Veronica's. When I'm satisfied that you're alone, only then will I call my men, giving them the heartbreaking news not to rape your little girl. How's that?"

I swallowed back the bile that rushed up to my throat. "Okay. I'll be there in five minutes."

"I can come with you if you like?" said Chris.

"No."

"What will I say to the cops?"

"Tell them everything that you know about Jessica. I've got to go." I jumped in the car and raced off.

I pressed the button on my console and called James. "Did you get a trace on that call?"

"Got it," said James.

"Okay. Get there now. Clarissa's been abducted by a couple of heavies. Hurry."

"We're onto it right now. She's on Sunset Boulevard."

"That figures. Fucking Jessica Mansfield. I'll be there as soon as I can. I have to meet her at Veronica's first. It's only up the road from there. Call the cops as a backup."

"We're onto it, Aidan."

As I sprinted along to the fashionable diner, my legs were heavy. In my mind, a warped motion picture of a million scenarios played out. I saw hairy, heavy dudes all over my angel. I wanted to fucking scream. The fire that was ablaze in my body and mind made me blind to the busy street of onlookers. Luckily, I had shades on.

I spotted Jessica sitting outside with a martini. About right for the lush that she was. Always had been. A spoiled little rich girl who'd taken so many drugs and alcohol she'd become deranged. I couldn't believe she'd resort to abduction, not to mention hiring a hitman.

An oily curl formed on her plumped pout. "That was quick."

"So this is your way? In order to get me, you're going to resort to criminal behavior. You're going to prison. I'll see to it."

"No, I won't. Daddy will save the day. He always does."

"You're seriously fucked up, Jessica. You have to have what you can't have. When you had me, you went around fucking anybody with that loose cunt of yours."

She winced. "Ooh... you're being nasty now. Michael's cock's dripping with the need to fuck your little girl."

I grabbed her wrist. "Listen, you fucking whore. If anything happens to Clarissa, if they touch her in any way, I will fucking rip you apart myself."

She laughed. "Mm... that sounds promising. You're so sexy when you're angry."

"What happens now? I want Clarissa freed. I'm here like you asked."

"We'll go home and have a nice fuck right in front of your little chick."

"What makes you think I can get hard around you? It was difficult enough when we were together."

"Ouch. Now you're being an asshole." Her green eyes narrowed as she licked her lips. "I'm the queen of blowjobs, darling. I remember drinking you up morning, noon, and night."

I couldn't believe that this woman was to be my wife once upon a time. Although she was beautiful in a manicured way, that self-entitled arrogance and hardness of heart made her detestable and ugly.

I stood up. "Let's go, then."

She dropped a large bill on the plate, finished her drink in one gulp, and followed me.

A message pinged on my phone. I stopped to read it. It was from James.

We're at the house. It's a fortress. We're trying to break in. Dogs everywhere. We've called the cops for backup.

Jessica stood close. "Put that away, sweetheart. We'll take my car."

"No. You've been drinking. I'll drive."

"Whatever," she said, holding onto my arm. "Mm... this is just like old times."

I shrugged violently out of her hold. "No, it's not. You can't force someone to be with you, Jessica."

She laughed. I could see she was enjoying herself. She was fearlessly insane. Experience had taught me that that was the most dangerous kind of criminal.

CHAPTER TWENTY-ONE

CLARISSA

His eyes were all over me. I'd already vomited. The other guy, who was a fraction kinder, pushed away the evil one, who'd already squeezed my breasts and bottom. Sleaze dripped from his beady black eyes. I wished I could make myself invisible. I recoiled at the way his hungry eyes ate me up. I'd even seen him rub himself with his hand. Somewhere at the back of my mind, I knew Aidan would save me. He had to.

My nerves were so tight I'd lost the ability to breathe properly. I had pins and needles from my icy veins not allowing blood to flow.

I wasn't sure who was behind this, but I imagined they wanted cash for me.

The same thought rotated in my mind—why, oh why, did I leave my bag in the car?

The gentler of the two men gave me some water, and because I was tied up, he placed a straw in the bottle so I could drink it hands-free. My throat was extremely dry, and my mouth was so bitter that the water tasted like a sugary drink.

Because they'd blindfolded me getting there, I had no idea what sort of place I was in. At least I was on a comfortable chair and not thrown in a dungeon. That was a small mercy, I supposed. It still didn't stop my body from shivering.

I heard a woman laughing, then a man's voice. It sounded like Aidan.

The door swung open, and in waltzed Jessica.

While she ran her icy green eyes up and down my body, Aidan ran over to me.

"Clarissa, my sweetheart. I'm sorry." He went down to hold me but was dragged back by her two henchmen.

Struggling out of their arms, Aidan pushed one away while the other positioned his fist and was about to strike Aidan when Jessica intervened.

"Leave him," she said. "Don't want to sully his gorgeous features. I don't want to see a bruised face eating my pussy." She cast an evil eye at me.

It was my turn to clench my fists. I'd never in my short life entertained the type of violent thoughts that had entered my mind. Her sniggering smile sent blood charging through me.

She sniffed the air. "Mm... I do like to fuck a man when he's sweaty. The smell of adrenaline is such a turn on." She undid her blouse and revealed a skimpy green bra that barely covered her heavy breasts.

Tears poured down my face. I could see Aidan's face had sunk into a deep frown. Sorrow reflected off his darkened eyes. He bent down and managed to hold me without being charged at this time. I figured that Jessica got off on seeing my heart torn apart.

"Words cannot express how deeply sorry and troubled I am at the moment." He pulled away to study my face. His sullen glower pretty much summed up how I felt. "Have they touched you?" His edgy rasp told me that he would do whatever it took to protect me.

But what about him? Was he about to fuck Jessica? I would have preferred a beating than having to endure that. Especially if his glorious cock went hard and needy, just as it did with me. That would destroy everything.

He faced me, waiting for a response from me. My soul went frigid. My mouth opened, but a lump in my throat swallowed back my words. I just shook my head slightly.

"She wants me to..." He exhaled a deep jagged breath. "You know you're the only one, Clarissa. I love you more anything. Remember that."

"Come on, lover boy. Show me that nice, big, fat cock. I'm all sticky and hot," she said, fanning her face.

I closed my eyes. I wanted to block my ears, but my hands were tied. My whole body felt as if it had been put in a refrigerator. Our perfect, fairy-tale romance was about to be defiled.

She grabbed Aidan by the crotch. This woman was a virago, a she-devil.

I squeezed my eyes tight.

"You're a fucking whore, Jessica," Aidan spat out.

"Tut, tut, tut. Do you want your little princess to be violated? I wouldn't mind watching that. Brendan is all hot and raring to go. And he's hung like a horse. He'll rip her apart."

A loud grunt stretching to a roar escaped Aidan's lips. He punched the wall above Jessica's head, putting a hole in it.

She laughed. "Let me see. Did you hurt yourself?" Jessica went to grab his hand, but Aidan moved away so violently that she stumbled back. Instead of anger, her face lit up with a malicious grin.

Jessica kneeled, then I heard her unzipping Aidan's jeans. Bile rose to my throat. I was about to retch. I didn't have anything left, and my stomach was struggling with convulsions. Much to my misery, my hearing was so acute I could hear every little sound, including jeans being unbuttoned and lowered.

"Mm...we'll have this big boy boning up in no time."

There was a sudden sound of commotion. The door fell crashing to the ground.

The next few moments played out like a scene from a badly choreographed fight scene in a movie. Aidan pushed Jessica to the floor and pulled up his pants.

When one of the heavies went for Aidan, he retaliated with a punch that was so hard, I heard a sickening crack.

James, along with two other men, managed with ease to hold one of the men down, while pushing Jessica down onto a sofa.

She uttered something smart-mouthed back at him.

The evil one of her two henchmen pulled out a gun. I screamed. Luckily, Aidan's reflexes were alerted in time, and he knocked the weapon out of the big brute's hand.

While the scuffles continued with men rolling around on the floor, Jessica scrambled to her feet and grabbed a vase.

Having managed to knock out Mr. Evil, Aidan stood with his back to her when she lunged for him.

I yelled, "Watch out!"

He turned in time and grabbed her wrist. The vase fell and shattered on the ground just as the police entered.

The first thing Aidan did was undo the ties around my hands. He rubbed my wrists while his hardened gaze softened. His lips tightened into a relieved smile before he took me into his arms, crushing me with love, almost.

"It's okay. You're safe now, baby. We're safe."

Pounding fast, my heartbeat vibrated in my ears.

"Clarissa, I can do this alone if you're not up to it," said Aidan as we drove to the police station.

"No, I want to get it over and done with. It involved me. I want to press charges." My tone was cold and resolute, which was pretty much how I felt. Something was raging within me. Resentment churned up dirt around my jaded being—my soul, muddied and murky.

Aidan glanced over at me as he steered the car. "What's up? Why do I get this feeling you're pissed off at me?"

I turned my head and stared out the window. The view of LA from Sunset Boulevard was predictably photogenic. Had I been less disturbed, I would have indulged in that ripple of delight I got from sunsets. But at that moment, it all looked gloomy and colorless.

"Clarissa," persisted Aidan.

"Not now, Aidan. Please. I can't talk."

CHAPTER TWENTY-TWO

It was hard to know what disturbed me more, knowing that Jessica had hired a professional hitman to kill me, or that Aidan attacked his bottle of bourbon as if he were drinking water for an unquenchable thirst.

The fact that I hadn't uttered a word since the police station probably had something to do with it. An orchestra of misgivings played a series of disharmonious tunes, layering and confusing me, stealing any kind of reasonable thought pattern. All my synapses were frozen, ripped apart even, disabling thoughts from moving with ease—as if the lights had literally gone out in my brain. My heart was a tiny little tight ball that barely moved. If anything, I needed to sleep so that I could escape myself.

I headed for the bathroom and grabbed the bottle of sleeping pills I'd spied earlier in the cabinet. I sprinkled two little tablets into my palm.

"They're strong. Take only one. You're not used to them," said Aidan, who had done nothing but follow me from the moment we'd arrived back.

I swallowed one pill and chased it with a palmful of water from the basin.

A large bath of hot water awaited me. I disrobed and tested the water with my hand. In better times, Aidan would jump in with me. His muscular thighs would wrap around me while his heavy erection, hot and ready, pushed impatiently against my skin.

"Is that a good idea, Clarissa, with the sedative?"

I shrugged.

"Please talk to me." His eyebrows drew in tight.

"Aidan, I have nothing to say at the moment. I'm kind of barren." A tear rolled down my face.

He held me, but instead of melding into his big frame and regaling in his masculine form, as my body normally did, I was frigid and tight. Aidan removed his arms.

"I love you so much, it hurts. I have never loved anyone as I love you, Clarissa. Without you, I can't function. I'm just as fragile and vulnerable as you, if not more. The love I feel for you has made me that way."

"Then I'm not good for you if I make you that fragile."

He combed back his mess of hair. "That's not what I meant." He touched his heart. "You're a part of me, Clarissa Moone. We're sewn at the hip, the heart, and the soul."

A tear chased the other. My eyes drank his softened blue gaze. Their enchantment radiated through to my body, which had started to thaw. How could a man be even more beautiful when torn? Aidan, with that mess of hair from his incessant fingering, made my heart melt.

"That's how I feel too, Aidan. I can't breathe without you. But I also couldn't breathe seeing Jessica touching you."

Aidan pulled down his pants and lifted his T-shirt over his head. He approached the bath. His hard, naked body, combined with the heat of the bath, had relaxed the noisy confusion in my mind. The sedative helped. I made room for him in the bath.

"That's what she wanted to do. She wanted to tear us apart," he said as he lowered himself into the water.

He took me in his arms and kissed my cheek. This time, my body softened into his big, strong arms.

My heart unraveled and started to pump warmth around my veins again.

I licked my lips to accommodate Aidan's crushing mouth, which expressed the desperation of one who'd almost lost something overwhelmingly close.

The sedative, the heat of the bath, and Aidan's big, beautiful frame holding me sent a reassuring and divine ache through my body.

My back fell sedately into Aidan's arms as he wrapped his strong thighs around me.

"Let's get married tomorrow, then we'll go to Europe the next day," he said with that sexy rasp that tickled my ear.

"No. Let's do it properly. I've got a beautiful dress. I like the idea of seeing photos of me in it and you looking all dishy in a tux."

He laughed. "Yes, something to show to all our children."

I pulled away and looked at him. "All our children? How many do you want?"

He shrugged. "As many as you want, princess. I must admit the thought of a large-brown-eyed little cutie running around sends shivers of warmth through me."

"Will you still want me after I've had babies? I've heard that a woman's body changes."

Aidan stroked my hair, and my heavy head fell onto his shoulder. "I will love you and desire you forever, Clarissa. Of that, I am more than certain."

My eyes struggled to stay open. I slurred, "That's nice."

· · · · ●· ● · · ·

THE NEXT DAY I awoke and found Tabitha sitting by the bed. I looked up at the French clock on the mantel and saw that it was midday. My eyelids were heavy, and I felt groggy.

"Hey, sleepyhead," she said with a large smile, placing a tray of coffee and muffins down by the bed.

I sat up and rubbed my eyes. "Shit. It's really late. I don't think I've ever slept this late. Where's Aidan?"

"He had to go to the police station. He dropped in first thing this morning and asked if I'd come over and babysit his favorite gal. And mine too." She was as ebullient as always. Like darkened eyes to sunlight, I had to adjust my sleepy brain to accommodate her exuberance.

"Oh?" I sat up and placed cushions against my back. I was naked and looked about for something to put on."

"Shit, Clary. I forgot how huge your tits were. No wonder Aidan can't keep his hands off you."

I had to laugh. "Can you pass me that T-shirt over there, please?"

Tabitha picked up Aidan's Led Zeppelin T-shirt off the chair and handed it to me.

As I slipped it over my head, a whiff of Aidan flitted up my nose, sending an immediate whoosh of heat through me. It was the first morning since moving in with Aidan that we hadn't made love. My body complained, especially with that addictive scent dazzling my senses.

"Thanks for the coffee." I leaned over to the tray. My stomach rumbled. I realized I hadn't eaten anything much the previous day.

I took a blueberry muffin and bit into it. Oozing warm, runny jam tantalized my taste-buds. It was almost as good as sex.

"Yum, I'm starving."

"Good to see." Tabitha took one, as well. "Wow, they're yummy, all right."

"Cooked here daily. Can you imagine how fat I'm going to get?"

"You're not fat, Clary. If anything, you've lost weight, except for your boobs. They've gained. I think you're the envy of every female in the world."

I giggled. I was glad she was there.

"Did Aidan tell you what happened?"

"Yep. That's why he dropped in. It was great timing," she said with a wry grin.

"Let me guess, you and Grant were at it?"

She nodded with a twinkle in her eyes. "It just gets better, Clary. He's fucking hot sex on tap."

"Okay, okay. Tell me about that later. But first, tell me about Aidan coming over."

"Yeah, well, he looked as if he'd had a big night. Grant could see he needed him, so I left them to it. But Aidan asked me to stay. Which I liked, you know? It made me feel like I was part of the family."

"You *are* part of the family. Aidan probably drank too much last night. That's why he looked the way he did. I was knocked out by a sedative."

"I know. Fuck, Clary. What an ordeal. Aidan told us all about it." She took a sip of her coffee and touched my hand. "Are you okay now?"

"I suppose so. I was pretty freaked out last night. But a bath and a sleeping pill kind of helped me regain some sense of proportion. I mean, for a while there, I went haywire. My mind did. Aidan said some bone-melting things, and slowly, I came back."

"He loves you madly, Clary. All he did this morning was pace in our kitchen, combing his hair back with his hands and talking about what he would've done if they'd touched you. Fuck, he's intense. Just like his hot dad."

I could just see him doing that and smiled. "Did he tell you that Jessica tried to make him fuck her in front of me?"

Her lips twisted downward. "Uh-huh." She shook her head. "Fuck, she sounds really twisted."

I sighed deeply. "She's seriously still in love with him. I can understand it. He's like nothing else. In fact, half of the time, I feel like I'm tripping or that I'm in some film that has an extended happy ending."

Tabitha laughed. "Speaking of fairy tales, there's your wedding, which is now only four weeks away. What about if the service is under the arch, with the roses creeping around it? Just like your father's wedding. Since you want a garden service."

I nodded thoughtfully. "Yeah, it's hard to surpass. In the rose garden. I love it there. It's where Aidan first asked me out."

"Really?"

"It wasn't really a date as such. A bit more organic than that. It was so sweet." I smiled, reliving our first time, as I'd done on so many occasions. It was as though there was a happy switch in my mind. When I needed a hit, I'd bring up the scene of Aidan and those breathtaking turquoise eyes. Not to mention his lips, which were like magnets for mine.

"He asked me to go for a walk with him, and before I knew it, I was having dinner on his yacht." I cocked a brow.

"And he took your innocence."

My body liquefied with warm, fuzzy feelings as I replayed the magical night. But then every night with Aidan sent the same shivery sensations sweeping through me.

"The garden it is. And for catering, I'll talk to Will."

"I'm just looking forward to wearing that dreamy thirties dress."

Tabitha stretched her arms. "I can't wait to see you in it, Clary." Her eyes sparkled with contagious excitement. My good friend had managed to sweep the cobwebs from the previous day's drama away.

CHAPTER TWENTY-THREE

AIDAN

"Hey, Kieren, thanks for seeing me quickly." I stepped through the door that he held open for me.

"That's what I'm here for." He stretched out his arm. "Go on through."

I lowered myself onto the armchair, and immediately, my muscles relaxed into the comfortable cushions. As always, whenever I visited that room, my eyes zeroed in on the colorful fish swimming behind the glass tank. I reminded myself to arrange for a large tank to be installed at the estate. If only to give my mind, which tended to overthink, a meditative focus. Art did that for me most of the time, but the floaty little exotic creatures took me somewhere else.

Kieren sat down. "I read about the abduction. It was in the media."

I scratched my prickly jaw, which was crying out for a razor. "Yeah, the goddamn circus is out and about. I tried to keep it out of the spotlight, but with the police involved, it's not possible." I exhaled a tight breath. "John Mansfield, Jessica's father, cornered me, and with that dogged businessman persistence, tried to make me agree not to press charges, even though that's up to Clarissa. He promised he'd send Jessica overseas for a long stint. He assured me he'd deal with her his own way."

"You don't sound too pleased with that arrangement," said Kieren.

"You got that right." I sat forward and rested my chin on my hands. "When I was in the Forces, I had to make decisions on the spot. Decisions that had life-or-death consequences. But in the war zone of love and romance, I'm in a fucking haze. My training has gone out the window. I'm just a muddled mess."

"I take it you left it open for the moment."

"I did. I need to discuss it with Clarissa first. It will be her decision in the end, though I suspect she'll probably leave it up to me, because being the kind-hearted soul that she is, Clarissa will find it difficult to press charges. For a moment there, after hearing Mansfield's proposal, I was fine with the idea of sending Jessica off and strapping an order against her not to approach Clarissa or me, but then, as she was leaving, she gave me this smug look. Which pretty much suggested that she hadn't finished with me yet."

"She's determined."

"Jessica's a deranged drug-addict. She's a spoiled brat who has had everything given to her all her life. If she can't have something, it becomes her obsession. I'll do my utmost to get Clarissa to press charges." I sighed loudly.

"Your voice is filled with dread, Aidan. It's the right thing to do, though. She had murderous intentions."

"I totally agree. But it's the court hearing and media frenzy. And it will go on and on. All my dirty laundry on display to the world. I couldn't give a shit about me. It's Clarissa that I'm trying to protect here. She's such a sweet, sensitive girl, and to be dragged through this bullshit..."

"I can understand your predicament. What about Clarissa? Have you asked her how she feels about pressing charges?"

I shook my head. "I'm trying not to bring it up. She's teetering on the verge of leaving me, I think."

"What gives you that impression? The gossip columns show constant images of love between you. I can see it in her eyes."

"You've seen those?" I was unable to hide my surprise. Kieren was a pipe-and-Hemingway kind of man, similar to Julian.

"You forget I have an eighteen-year-old daughter." He cocked his head.

I nodded. "Clarissa was so cold and withdrawn last night. I felt that she was blaming me. And to be honest, it *is* my fault. If I hadn't been with Jessica, all of this wouldn't be happening. Clarissa was also the victim of an incident on the highway that nearly took her life. Jessica hired a hitman to kill Clarissa."

Kieren sat up, his brow lowered. "That's very serious. Clarissa must be traumatized by all this. Anybody would be."

I nodded. "She is. I've tried everything to get her to a counselor or to visit you, but she doesn't want to. Instead, she has her close friend, Tabitha, who she talks to about everything, I suspect."

"You told me that her mother died in a car accident that Clarissa was a passenger in. And that she didn't speak for a year after that."

"Yeah, poor baby," I said. "You know, it's not indecision about Jessica that brings me here, even though I wouldn't mind getting your thoughts on that. It's this rage that's burning inside of me. I wanted to knock Jessica out. Even when she tossed me that smarmy, I-get-whatever-I-want gaze, my fists were so tight, I had to use all my inner strength not to hit her."

"Are you frightened that you might try to hurt her?"

I exhaled a tight breath. "When I was in that room with her, I squeezed every ounce of self-control I could muster. I ended up putting a hole in the wall above her head."

He peered down at my knuckles and noticed the bruising. "But you didn't, which proves your cut-off switch is functioning."

"Yeah, well, sort of, I suppose. It causes tightness in my chest that hurts. But look, I just needed to speak honestly about it to someone. I can't tell Clarissa that I wanted to knock Jessica out, because I don't want her to get the impression that I'm one of those uncultivated brutes."

"It's instinct, Aidan, that desperate need to protect those we love dearly. The primal survival mechanism in the brain doesn't distinguish between gender. As it is, Jessica was threatening Clarissa." He paused to reflect. "Tell me, what did she make you do?"

My back stiffened. "She wanted me to have sex with her in front of Clarissa."

His brows drew in tight. "That's wielding an ax, for sure. Had it taken place it would have strained your relationship. I take it you didn't get that far?"

I shook my head. "To be honest, I was flaccid. But she was about to blow me." I shifted awkwardly. It felt as if I were confessing something sordid to an old relative. "You know how the male anatomy is when it's coaxed."

"One does hear of females raping males. It's not common, but it happens."

"Anyway, it didn't, thank God. My wedding's four weeks away."

"Oh good, you've made a date."

"You didn't get the invite?" I asked.

He shook his head.

"I'll get onto it. I'd love you to come along with your family, and for you to finally meet Clarissa. I only hope..."

"You only hope?"

"It goes ahead."

"Aidan, I'm sure it will. With regards to the media circus and getting Jessica put away... I, personally, would charge her. But do what you think best. Would her father be able to tame her?"

"He told me he'd cut off her funds. Jessica has lived a very privileged existence all her life, so I imagine that would be serious punishment."

"Well, then, you could try to risk it, I suppose. But she doesn't strike me as someone who'll stop harassing you."

"That's what I think. I have enough evidence to link her to the attempted murder. That alone would see her taken down." I stood up, feeling decisive and determined. "You know what? I'm going to make sure she has her day in court. I won't be able to rest, knowing that she could harm Clarissa again."

"I agree, Aidan. It's for the best."

I shook his hand. "Thanks for finding the time for me. And I look forward to seeing you at my wedding."

I sat in my car and made the call. My hand trembled. Media circus or not, Jessica was going to have her day in court. With Chris's testimony, no fancy lawyer would be able to get her off. Or at least I hoped. I even called Chris again to check to see if he was still on board. He was more than determined to help. He was very fond of Clarissa, and for once, I wasn't jealous.

When I returned home, I found Clarissa in the office with Tabitha. They'd been drafting the invites and were giggling and being rowdy.

I poked my head in, and Clarissa gazed up at me with her big, velvety eyes and smiled. Warmth swept through me.

Determined not to talk about Jessica and the police, I'd decided it was going to be our night.

"Can you include Kieren Tyler and his family in the invite list, baby?"

"Of course."

Tabitha looked up and said, "The more the merrier. I'm trying to convince Clary to have a big fat wedding."

I grinned. "I don't mind whichever way. As I long as you're there on the day, I don't mind who's watching."

Clarissa threw me one of her sultry looks, and I felt like myself again. She had that power over me. Her moods were my moods.

"I'm going up for a loud session with Ferrari. Dinner in an hour?"

Clary looked at Tabitha. "We should be done by then. Can Tabitha stay for dinner? And have James drive her home?"

"You bet." I looked at Tabitha and smiled.

"Thanks." She smiled sweetly.

• • • • • • • • • •

DURING DINNER, THERE WAS no talk of Jessica. Only the wedding plans and silly little banter about nothing much, which was what the doctor ordered. I was too weighed down to get into an intense discussion.

When I walked Tabitha to the gate, where James stood waiting, I said, "Hey, I'm really grateful that you came by to spend time with Clarissa."

"She's my sister. I'd do anything for her," she responded with a serious tone that I hadn't heard from her before.

"I know that. That's why I came to you. Has she said anything? I mean, is she really okay?"

"She told me everything that happened. She was pretty freaked out. But I reminded her that you were the catch of the century and that you'd protect her."

I laughed. "Thanks for that."

"Anytime. And look, I hope that you're okay over the Brad thing in New York," she said.

"I stopped judging people's bedroom behavior a long time ago. I'm a possessive, jealous, and some would say controlling man. I could never be with a woman who played around. My father, however, is a different beast."

She nodded. "Thanks, Aidan. That makes me feel better. Grant knows. I told him. I couldn't tell how he felt about it, though. He's hard to read in that way. In any case, he lives in the present. He doesn't look back or too far forward."

"That's my dad. He's a day-by-day sort of guy. I'm not sure where my need to know and control the future comes from."

"We're all individuals, Aidan. We're not our parents."

I nodded slowly. "No, we're not."

On that note, I kissed Tabitha on the cheek and left her with James.

I sprinted back to my angel, who I hoped would be waiting for me pantyless so that I could ravage her.

My mother entered my thoughts causing my legs to stiffen. What was I going to do about her? She'd hear about the wedding and probably crash it in that forceful way of hers, causing a ruckus.

I cooked up a plan to offer her a holiday in the Bahamas or, more to her taste, an extended stay in Las Vegas. Or I could just have her at the wedding, acting in her drunken, loudmouthed manner, making the guests grimace and whisper amongst themselves. The thought of which, for some twisted reason, made me laugh.

I found Clarissa on the chaise longue, reading, an image that nourished my spirit and always brought a smile to my face.

She wore a silk gown that my fingers craved to undo so that I could touch her warm, softness.

Clarissa must have sensed my burning gaze. She looked up, and her eyes glistened from sweet to sultry in a blink. Moving over, she made room for me.

We gazed into each other's eyes, and all the drama from the previous day evaporated.

My hand caressed her shoulder, then traveled down to her waist and untied the silky gown. It dripped off her. My hands landed on a lacy little number that barely covered that cock-swelling body.

I left a trail of kisses along her soft neck all the way to her soft lips. She tasted of cherries.

A fire built furiously. I was going to come on the spot.

I lifted her in my arms and placed her on the bed. "You look scrumptious," I murmured, removing my clothes.

My cock was so hard that it ached.

Running her tongue over her lips, Clarissa gazed at my throbbing cock. She was just as hungry as I was. *Good.*

"Do you want me to turn, you know on all fours?" she asked with that breathy, aroused voice that was making my balls blue.

"Baby, I'll take you any way. But yeah, sure. Do you like it that way?"

She nodded with a shy little smile. That was the end of me. I turned her over, ripped off her lace panties, and tongued her until she trembled in my arms and spurted cream into my mouth. She tasted like honey.

I couldn't wait. I pushed the head of my cock into her. As always, it was a struggle to get in. But boy, it was a struggle my cock loved and couldn't get enough of.

Inching into her, I took it slowly.

"You're so fucking tight, it's almost torture," I said, barely able to talk properly.

"I'm sorry," she said, a moan kissing my ear as I inched in deeper.

"Don't be sorry, Angel. You feel fucking exquisite. Like nothing I've ever experienced before."

Her ass pushed hard against my balls. That was enough for me. My cock thrust in so deeply I hit a spot that made her cry out. I could not tell if it was pain or pleasure.

"Are you okay?"

"Go hard, Aidan, please."

That breathy voice added to the erotic package that was Clarissa. A serious eruption brewed.

It only took a few thrusts and the tension that had ransomed my body disappeared. Stars exploded behind my eyes, a savage groan grew louder and louder, as I emptied deeply into the love of my life.

I fell on my back, my heart pounding against my chest. My darling by my side, equally breathless.

We stared at the ceiling, waiting to regain our senses.

I took Clarissa into my arms. "Sorry, that was so quick. In the morning. Promise."

"It was perfect. Just like you, Aidan."

I kissed her deeply, drinking from her lips the elixir I needed for a peaceful rest.

We fell asleep with our bodies enfolded together as one.

CHAPTER TWENTY-FOUR

CLARISSA

WHAT AN IMAGE AIDAN made, walking about shirtless with his jeans unbuttoned as he looked for his phone. I lounged back and enjoyed the show, every delicious sinew flexed and powering along, his rippling abs and those large, muscular arms that had crushed me with affection earlier.

He glanced at me. "What?"

I shrugged. "You look so damn sexy like that, shirtless and your butt in those jeans."

He smiled sweetly. "Are you objectifying me, Clarissa Moone?"

"Yes, you could say that. But it's for your benefit because you make me all creamy when I see you like that."

He stopped what he was doing. "Clarissa, I've seriously got to go, and I've lost my phone. You're making me hard again."

The phone buzzed. It had fallen under the covers. I bent forward and picked it up. "Here it is."

"Thanks, princess." He took it from me, passing me one of his knock-out twinkly-eyed smiles.

"Thornhill," he said in his deep professional voice.

I sat up and watched him. He turned his back to me and ran his fingers through his hair, which told me that it was serious.

"All right. Sure. I'll be there."

He turned. His eyes had gone dark.

I swallowed. "What?"

"It's Chris." He looked stunned. "They've found him dead."

My body sprang up, and my jaw fell open. "What? How?" I jumped out of bed.

"A needle. They found a needle in his arm. He overdosed. The police went there to get a statement about Jessica, and that's how they found him."

"Oh my God, Aidan. It's foul play. I know it is."

He nodded. "Yeah, that's the first thing that hit me. Look, I've got to go now."

I was looking for my clothes. My head was swimming in a million directions. Tears were pouring down my cheeks. "I want to come with you, Aidan."

"No, baby, please. This is messy shit. They need me to look at the body. He's got no family." His face was a crumpled mess, a mirror of my emotions.

Tears continued to fall freely on my face. Aidan came and held me.

"I know. He was a good guy. Such a fucking talent, such a fucking waste." He pulled away. His face had gone red. "If Jessica's behind this, I'll make sure they slam her away and throw away the fucking key."

"Aidan, it is her. I'm convinced. Chris admitted to me once that he dabbled in heroin. But he assured me that he was always really careful with it and, unlike other junkies, didn't shoot up all the time."

"Yeah, he said something like that to me, too. Look, baby, I have to run. I'll call you. I promise."

He pulled a T-shirt over his head and left in a hurry.

After that, I remained frozen like a zombie all day. All I could do was sit on the balcony and stare out onto the grounds and to the sea as though seeking counsel from nature. One thing was for sure, I was glad to be staring at trees and not the grimy backstreets of LA.

When my phone buzzed, I jumped. I lifted my heavy body and looked down at the screen, which showed Aidan's beautiful face as the phone vibrated.

"Hey."

"Hey, princess." He took a deep breath. "I'm still at the station. I'm waiting for the detective."

"Did you see him?" I asked, my voice betraying a tremor.

"Yeah. It wasn't pretty. Although..."

"What?" I asked.

"He looked peaceful and not it any pain. Strange." He sniffed. "Chris had that look he always pulled when poking his tongue out at people. Do you know the look I mean?"

"You mean that I-don't-give-a-shit expression of his?" My voice broke, and a lump settled in my throat.

"Yeah, that one. Fuck." His voice trembled.

"Aidan, do you think he was murdered?"

"I've heard they've already cleaned up the scene. I don't know. I think the cops are in on it."

"What do you mean?"

"Just that. They don't want to do an autopsy. They're convinced he overdosed. When I asked about the syringe, they just dismissed it."

"No autopsy? But that's not right. Aren't they meant to?"

"According to the head cop, the fact that Chris was a junkie didn't justify an autopsy. They said that they don't have that kind of funding. I offered to pay for one. But they said that only family could arrange it and I'm not family."

"Hell." I found myself suddenly frustrated and angry about how society judged people too quickly, and unfairly.

"Did he mention any family to you?" asked Aidan.

"I asked once. He said he was an only child and that his mother and father were dead. In a fire, I think."

The line went dead.

"Are you there, Aidan?"

"Yeah." He sighed. "Look, Clarissa, I have to go. Hudson's arrived. I'll speak to you as soon as I've spoken to him, okay, beautiful girl?"

"Okay. I love you, Aidan."

He drew a sharp breath in. "And I love you more than anything in this world, angel."

CHAPTER TWENTY-FIVE

AIDAN

"PULL UP A SEAT," the detective said.

I jumped straight into it. "I believe Chris Wilde was murdered."

He nodded slowly. "Probably."

I shrugged and held my hands out. "What does that mean?"

"Look, Aidan, I've spoken to the chief of police. They're not taking it further."

"But you agree it was foul play."

The older man, whose face had more lines than a map, looked back at me with a deadpan expression.

I wasn't going to take that poker-faced nothingness as an answer. I sat forward. "Did they analyze the syringe for fingerprints?"

"Aidan, I believe it's a closed case. The department doesn't like spending money on junkies."

"Chris was more than a fucking junkie." My voice trembled. "He was probably one of the country's finest artists. I've seen plenty, and the guy had fucking talent dripping off him. He also helped a bunch of vets by inspiring them out of their torn shells to create great art. He has done more for this country than many that I know of."

He nodded slowly. "We can't do an autopsy unless there's some evidence of tampering. Or unless his family demands it. He has no family, Aidan."

I removed a checkbook from my pocket. "How much do you want? I'll pay for it."

"Put it away. It's not going to happen." There was something in his face that showed frustration.

"Why? What do you know, Detective? Look, if I have to hire my own private dick, I will, you know? I already contracted one when that body washed up."

"Yeah, that was timely. The FBI had a file this long on him." His arm stretched out.

"A hitman, yeah, and we know who hired him, don't we?" My tone had gone acrid.

"That's impossible to prove."

"Why? I mean, you knew this dude was a contracted killer. Surely you've been able to study his digital footprint."

"That's the FBI. They're not letting us in on it. But I can tell you he covered his tracks well. Have you heard of the deep, dark web?"

"Of course, I have. Drug dealers, sleazy assholes like pedophiles and the like," I said.

"It's more than that. There are all kinds of sons of bitches in there, plying and peddling their nasty wares. Including hitmen. That's where they get their contracts. It's so complex that even the FBI can't crack it."

"Are you telling me you have nothing on Jessica Mansfield? Apart from the kidnapping incident. You've got evidence of that, don't you? Or has that been whitewashed, as well?" Rage burned in my voice.

He stared at me long and hard. In his eyes, I saw an empty shell of a man who I suspected had seen it all and had chosen a cave to park his emotions.

"I'm going to tell you something, Aidan. It didn't come from me."

"What?"

"John Mansfield's got the head of the LAPD on his payroll. He's one of those seriously rich guys that can buy himself and his daughter out of trouble."

"Well then, I'm one of those fucking seriously rich guys who can and *will* buy fucking justice." I slapped his desk.

My eyes remained locked on his dismissive, weakened visage. Dogged determination impelled me to stay put. I wasn't leaving that office until I was given something.

He nodded pensively. "Fingerprints had been wiped on the syringe."

His eyes pierced me with something hard to read. Finally, he gave me a way in.

"Then what are we going to do, Detective? Do I have to bring in my own investigator? Or are you happy to take my cash and deliver justice the way it should be delivered—honestly? Surely that's why you exist in this role—to bring down crooked assholes?"

His lips turned up at one side. "That's why I joined. But this place is littered with crooked cops, all the way up. I know that well enough. I also know that John Mansfield has plenty of blood on his greasy, well-manicured hands. He's involved with a cartel from Columbia. He's my little secret mission. Secret because the department will shut it down if it knows I'm casing him."

I opened the checkbook and wrote a check for fifty thousand dollars. "Here, for your campaign. But you must promise to find the fucker that killed Chris."

He took the check and looked at it for a long while before passing it back to me. "No. I don't want it. I don't need it. I joined the police force for good. I don't want to be like those assholes on the take."

I took the check back. "I want his head on a block, Detective." I stood up. "I will not stop until he and that daughter of his have their day in court."

Hudson stretched back his arms. "Leave it to me. I've got a few contacts and a few good cops on my side."

I rose. "I want to arrange a proper funeral for Chris."

He stared at me for a moment, as if he was trying to figure me out. "You'll have to arrange that through the mortuary. I'll get those details to you later today."

· · · ● · ● ● · · ·

CHRIS'S STUDIO WAS CRAMMED with wall-to-wall people. I'd decided to have the service there. At first, Clarissa tried to convince me to have it at a chapel, but I argued that Chris was too much of an atheist and that he'd be pissed off. Clarissa nodded with a faint smile as we recalled the late artist's scathing cynicism toward religion.

Dressed in a black dress that did nothing to hide her beauty, Clarissa came to me. She'd been working tirelessly, curating an exhibition of Chris's works to be hung in time for the service.

I held out my arm so that she could stand tight against me.

"I can't believe how many people there are," she said.

"I suppose word gets out quickly in these circles," I said, looking about. There were mainly women. Most of whom, I speculated, Chris had probably been intimate with.

"Hey, Aidan," said Roy, who was looking unslept and pale.

"Roy, how are you, man?" I asked.

His bloodshot eyes widened slightly. "I've been better. I liked Chris. Not just because he was my teacher, but he was a good guy. He had a big heart. He may not have shown it. He didn't do this, you know?"

I nodded. "Yeah, I know."

"He'd stopped shooting up. He told me that. He was smoking it instead," said Roy.

"I didn't know that. It would be useful if you gave a statement to the cops about that."

His face fired up for the first time. "Anything to catch the fucking prick who did this."

He bowed his head and shuffled off.

It was a moving service, with many declarations of respect and love for a man who claimed to be a lone wolf.

After the service, we took the ashes to Venice, where we scattered them out to sea.

The ride home was a silent one, which suited me. I wasn't good with funerals. I wasn't good with death. Period.

CHAPTER TWENTY-SIX

CLARISSA

"Is it too revealing?" I asked, standing in front of the mirror, moving my head from side to side.

"No, Clary. You look beautiful. It's so silky and gorgeous to the touch. Aidan's hands will be all over it in a flash, I'm sure." Tabitha smiled.

As always, sex entered the conversation. I didn't mind, because the thought of Aidan's needy hands all over me worked miracles at easing my nerves.

"And the way it pools to the ground with that little train," said Tabitha, stroking my wedding gown.

"I love the fall too. It's as if it were made for me. I didn't have to get it adjusted at all."

"It's perfect. And we've done a fine job with strapping those boobs. Holy shit, you actually almost look normal-sized."

I laughed, which hurt. I had a corset on, and it wasn't comfortable. Nevertheless, the excitement of the day did away with any physical discomfort.

Tabitha put the final touches on my Spanish bun that she'd expertly arranged to sit down on my neck. The beautiful chandelier diamond earrings dangled heavily off my ears. All that was left to do was to place the splendid antique lace veil on my head. We'd attached it to a tortoiseshell, diamante-encrusted hair comb like the Spanish women used to hold up their mantillas. It had actually belonged to my late Spanish grandmother, and for that reason it felt special.

It was such a flattering and feminine look that I'd always admired. I recalled when, as a young girl, I was taken to my grandmother's house for parties. All the women would dress in flamenco outfits. On their heads were high combs and flowers, and their hair combed back tight with long buns on their necks. That was when I fell in love with that style.

As I stared at myself in the mirror, tears welled up. I thought about my late mother, and how she would have loved seeing me looking like her mother, whom I looked exactly alike.

After placing the large comb on the top of my head, Tabitha pushed in some large hairpins to hold it in place. She took a few steps away from me and held her chin, studying me intently.

"You look just like a Spanish senorita from those fifties films we love."

"Good. That's how I want to look," I said.

I was as nervous as hell. This was it. I was to be married to the man who, every waking moment, made my heart and body swell with love and desire.

Greta entered the room, carrying a bouquet of creamy silk flowers. She stopped, and her face filled with wonder.

"Clarissa, you look so beautiful." She stroked the silk of my gown. "That is a genuine thirties dress. So tasteful, and very you. Aidan will be thrilled. I love the diamantes around the neckline, and I see they carry on around the dip in the back. Stunning."

"Thanks, Greta. You look great in that dress. Did you buy it in Europe?"

"I did. As soon as Aidan told me that we better be here for his birthday because that was going to be your wedding day, I made sure I went shopping in Paris."

"I love it. It really suits you, Greta. You look great, and so does Dad in his tux. How did you get him to wear it?" I laughed. My dad was not a conventional man when it came to wardrobe. "He's even wearing a bow tie."

"The bow tie was a battle," said Greta with a chuckle. "When he lunged for a purple one with red polka dots I had to take charge. It was probably the first argument we've ever had."

"I can imagine. Dad's always been eccentric when it comes to clothes."

"Hmm... now we know where you get it from," said Tabitha.

Greta turned to look at Tabitha. It wasn't a smile as such, just a subtle nod. I couldn't read how she'd taken the news that Tabitha was her twin brother's new wife to be. My stepmother-stroke-auntie-to-be, as always, was at her inscrutable best.

Greta handed me the antique bouquet of cream silk flowers with hanging ribbons and lace. "Here, Clarissa. These belonged to my mother, Aidan's grandmother."

"Oh, they're lovely. Thank you," I gushed.

Then the nerves really kicked in. As the bouquet balanced languidly in my palms, I was reminded that I really was about to become Clarissa Thornhill and that it wasn't some sexy dream.

"Okay, I will leave you to it," said Greta. "See you out there. Your father's nervous, but excited. He'll be here soon to take you."

"Thanks, Greta."

I turned to Tabitha. "My legs are wobbling."

"Take a walk around the room. Get used to the shoes. They're perfect. I love them."

"They're uncomfortable, Tabs." I looked down at my off-white ankle-strapped, open-toed sky-scrapper shoes. "I don't know how I'm going to walk onto the uneven grounds in them."

"Your dad will help you balance, then you can lean against Aidan's strong shoulders."

My heart pumped little butterflies through my body, making it tingle from all the fluttering.

"I can't believe this is happening," I said, my eyes welling up.

Tabitha held my hand and looked directly at me. "Don't you dare cry. You'll ruin my fantastic makeup job."

I giggled. "You did use waterproof, I hope."

"Of course. We can't have our girl looking like an ax-murdering clown."

I laughed. "Oh, Tabs. I'm so glad you're here with me. And you look gorgeous in that green dress."

She'd worn a slinky green silk dress with a little train to match my dress.

"Do you think so?" She stood before the mirror adjusting it to make a little cleavage show. "I'm glad you didn't go all bridezilla on me and expect me to wear a puffy dress that made it hard to distinguish me from the wedding cake."

We both looked at each other and broke into screeching laughter. Tabitha had done it again.

"Stop it, Tabs. I'm going to look like a wreck out there. And you better not pull any of your crazy faces at me. I'll kill you."

"Who are you going to kill?" said my father, stepping into the room. When he saw me, he stopped, and his dark eyes widened. "Oh, my darling Clarissa, you look so beautiful."

I fell into his arms. "Oh, Daddy. Please don't. You'll make me cry."

He stepped back and looked at me, shaking his head. "You are your mother. And I love that Spanish touch." He pointed to my hair comb. "Just like your grandmother, Esmeralda." He took a hanky out of his pocket and blew his nose. His handsome dark eyes glistened.

"You're looking sharp, Julian," said Tabitha.

He hugged her. "Oh, you think so? And you too, darling girl. Green's always been your color."

Tabitha smiled demurely. She was always that little girl around my dad.

"Okay, then, are we ready?" my father asked hooking his arm.

I slipped my arm around his. "Let's do it. On with the show. This is it," I sang, mimicking Aidan's childlike response to pomp and occasion.

It was quite a walk to the rose garden, especially taking the path and not the grounds to cut across, which was how I normally got there. But that was wearing sensible shoes.

"Can't I take them off until we get close?" I asked as I wobbled along.

"Oh, Clary, by now you should be able to sprint in them," said Tabitha. She had her arm linked with mine.

Between my father and Tabitha, I managed to move forward.

"They're ridiculously high," I said, tottering along. In truth, my nerves were wreaking havoc on my equilibrium. I was so relieved that my father would walk me down the aisle.

Aidan had arranged the music.

Devina Velvet, dressed in a wine-colored body-hugging gown, sparkled as always. Her presence in the rose garden was a natural fit. It was like a magical dream. By her side stood a stand-up bass, as curvaceous as she was, along with a seated guitarist and a man playing a shiny saxophone. From her sensual lips, a husky, sweet sound floated through the garden.

As she sang *Summer Breeze* it floated in the air like a smooth caress, making the fine hairs on my arm spike.

A saxophone solo sent curvy, sensual notes swirling through the air, that seemed to glide us along.

When we arrived, the guests' heads all turned together, fifty smiling people sighing, whispering, and generally aroused by the spectacle before them.

And a spectacle it was.

In the redolent, intoxicating rose garden, one didn't need champagne to feel light-headed.

My seriously handsome husband-to-be waited for me at the end of the aisle. His head turned with those eyes twinkling like the sea. Aidan was dressed in a heart-swelling tux that fitted his scrumptious, strong body so perfectly a silent moan left my lips.

I stepped onto the red carpet, my father holding my arm, while Tabitha arranged my veil to trail behind me.

A soft, swirly saxophone solo started the proceedings. It danced all the way up to Devina's velvety voice as her husky breath kissed the air while she sang, "It's very clear. Our love's here to stay."

Aidan was the prize. Our eyes locked. Everything around me was a blur. My legs weren't even there anymore. I was floating.

My mind, heart, and soul all asked the same question. "Is this really happening? Am I really going to be in that delicious man's arms forever?"

As I fell into Aidan's turquoise gaze, my beautiful late mother entered my thoughts. I thanked her, as I'd done often, for bringing joy into my life in the shape of that beautiful, sexy man whose heavy-lidded stare sizzled through me.

I was swept away in a sea of emotion. A big lump had parked itself in my throat.

It was an out-of-body experience, and I felt as if I were flying through the air. All I saw was my handsome husband-to-be dressed in a tux that left me breathless. His tall, strong body owned it to perfection.

A long, shaky breath left my lips, which were curling out of control as we continued to lock eyes. Aidan's hair, pomaded back gently, brushed his collar.

As I glided toward a destiny that promised everything and so much more, Devina crooned about our love lasting forever. Her stretched, impeccable, heartrending notes made my heart dance, especially with Aidan's eyes eating me up, reflecting belief.

Belief in us.

CHAPTER TWENTY-SEVEN

AIDAN

WAS THAT GRACEFUL BEAUTY really going to be mine forever? I asked myself as I indulged in a skin-tingling moment of the Gershwin tune that Devina Velvet sang almost as perfectly as the Ella Fitzgerald version I loved.

Dressed in that silky vintage dress that hugged those curves in a way my skin ached to do, Clarissa was a goddess. The veil framing her face, which had launched a thousand emotions in me, made her look like an angel.

And an angel she was. An angel that was to be mine forever.

All mine, forever.

As Clarissa glided toward me, I'd never been more certain of anything in my life. My heart grew so large that it felt naked and on show.

I didn't see anybody, except Clarissa.

She stepped by my side, and our hands clasped. Her little hand was hot and damp, the heat of which raced up my arm.

Adhering to tradition, Clarissa had insisted on a night apart. As a result, I'd had a restless night. But as she stood by my side, her hand in mine, I felt so energized that I could have run a marathon. Never before had I felt like that.

It was pure happiness.

As a natural pessimist, I'd never believed in such a thing before Clarissa entered my life. But at that moment, life was so good that I suddenly felt religious for the first time in my life. I believed there had to be a god for delivering to my soul, heart, and body the prize that was Clarissa Moone, soon to be Clarissa Thornhill.

"Will you take this woman, to have and to hold, in sickness and in health, for as long as you live?"

Not even a second passed before I uttered, "Yes," with such ironclad certainty that I felt like punching the air. Of course, I remained decorously still, even though my body was doing all kinds of strange things. And when Clarissa's beautiful lips parted with a breathy "Yes," not only did my soul sigh, but my cock got in on the action.

Shit.

I tried to grip the member with my legs. The last thing I needed was my pants tenting.

As I moved in to kiss Clarissa, I pressed against her. She felt it all right because she pushed against me. The kiss lingered. No tongues. This was a classy affair, after all. Just soft, hot, beautiful, soulful lips that still managed to send me flying to the moon

A sexy saxophone riff set it off spectacularly as our lips remained locked together. We released each other, and when the chanteuse began singing the opening words of "At Last" with her husky voice, we both nearly fell into each other's arms again.

I'd chosen Etta James's sultry song for what it meant to me. Because Clarissa had come to me after I'd lost hope of ever finding the kind of love great art had been raving about forever.

I looked down at my banded finger. It was a beautiful ring, not plain and ordinary, but florid with Celtic scrolls. I loved it sitting there on my finger as a testimony to the extraordinary, creative life Clarissa and I had before us.

"Aidan, I love this song," my angel said in a thick, emotion-gripped voice.

That song always did that to me. It was a risk having it there. But boy, it packed a punch, and it described me. It was melancholic in a hopeful want-to-embrace-life way.

"It's sad, though," she said.

I stopped and stared at her. I brushed her warm, wet cheek. "Beauty and love inspire so much feeling and emotion, it can seem sad. But not in a tragic way, in a heart-releasing way."

"Aidan, you're deep, sexy, and oh God, I'm so happy, I could cry. In fact, I am crying," she said, sniffling and laughing at the same time.

I passed her a hanky. "Here, princess. And Clarissa..."

She stared up at me with her large eyes. "Yes?"

"I have never seen a more stunning bride in my life. I can't wait to see the photos and I also can't wait to..." I held her in my arms.

"To do what, Aidan?" Her eyes sparkled with promise.

"I can't wait to see that gorgeous silky dress slink off that irresistible body, which is mine. All mine. Has always been and now, always will be."

"It is yours, Aidan. It always has been. Just as your scrumptious body is mine. All mine, forever and ever."

We both pulled away and looked at each other and laughed, more from the intensity of our words than anything else.

EPILOGUE

"AIDAN, HOW DID YOU arrange this?" Clarissa asked as we headed through the entrance of the Uffizi gallery.

"If there was one thing I learned last time I was in Italy, it was that one can get anything for the right sum of money."

"You paid someone to give us free rein of the museum?"

"I certainly did," I said, feeling pleased with myself. It hadn't exactly been that easy. In fact, I'd had to line the quality leather wallets of six people. But it was worth it. The exuberance bouncing off Clarissa's big eyes was definitely worth it.

"I didn't want men to hear my favorite girl oohing and aahing as if she were being entered by a hungry cock."

Clarissa giggled and slapped my arm. "You're a sex maniac, Aidan."

"Around you I am."

"In any case, I don't ooh and aah when I'm looking at art. Do I?"

I smiled. "You do, Clarissa. I've heard it over and over again. It's the most perfect sound on this planet. I recall you doing it the first night at the Gala event. Remember that, when I could hardly talk around you? I'm sure you thought I was stupid."

"You didn't appear stupid, Aidan. You just looked smoking hot, so much so, I babbled."

I laughed. "It was sexy, intelligent babble. That much I do remember." I stopped walking and turned to face her. "In truth, I remember every delicious second of it. I remember every moment I've spent with you, Clarissa. I often replay it in slow motion. Especially that first night on the yacht."

"Me too, Aidan," she said with a gentle smile.

Holding hands, we continued on, and within two steps, Clarissa was indeed oohing and aahing. It was music to my ears. I loved the reddening of her cheeks and girlish excitement that overtook Clarissa whenever she was surrounded by art.

I stood there, smiling, indulging in her beauty. She just grew more beautiful each day.

As we strolled along the ancient marble floor, the only sound, other than our footsteps, reverberating off the walls was Clarissa's sighs, leaving me to wonder if anybody had, in its four hundred fifty years, ever fucked in the Uffizi.

Mm...

There was always a first time for everything, I thought as I watched Clarissa's delightful butt swaying before me after I'd taken a step back to watch, as I always did.

Sensing my ogling, Clarissa turned and giggled. "Aidan, you should be looking at the art."

"I *am* looking at the art." I raised my brows.

Yes, life was great, greater than I could have imagined. Especially after I'd gotten a call from Detective Hudson, telling me that a new commissioner had been appointed to the LAPD and that Jonathon Mansfield had been tried and convicted for the murder of Chris Wilde.

The story had it that he'd sent in one of his men to inject Chris with the lethal dose that killed him. He tried to plead that he was protecting his daughter from slander. He also made up some half-cocked story that Chris had raped Jessica.

Jessica didn't get away either, much to my relief. She'd been convicted for kidnapping Clarissa. And although they couldn't pin the hit job on her, I was assured that the FBI was getting closer to finding out the dead hitman's contracts and who'd ordered them.

Clarissa pointed to a statue of Eros and Psyche. "It's magnificent. Enfolding lovers."

I opened my arms. "Just like us, my love. Come here and enfold me."

THE END

ALSO BY J J SOREL

A Taste of Peace
Devoured by Peace
It Started in Venice
The Importance of Being Wild
The Importance of Being Bella
Steamy Romantic Suspense
Take My Heart
Flooded
Flirted
Flourished
In League with Ivy
Steamy Dark/Gothic Romance
Dark Descent into Desire
Uncovering Love

jjsorel.com

Made in the USA
Columbia, SC
09 May 2023

16258425R10119